Abby Ann Judson

A happy year

Fifty-two letters to the Banner of light

Abby Ann Judson

A happy year
Fifty-two letters to the Banner of light

ISBN/EAN: 9783337270193

Printed in Europe, USA, Canada, Australia, Japan

Cover: Foto ©Andreas Hilbeck / pixelio.de

More available books at **www.hansebooks.com**

ABBY A. JUDSON.

OR,

Fifty-two Letters to The Banner of Light.

BY

ABBY A. JUDSON,

Daughter of ADONIRAM JUDSON, Missionary to the Burmese Empire.

PUBLISHED BY THE AUTHOR.

NEWARK, N. J.:
BAKER PRINTING CO.
1899.

THIS BOOK IS

Dedicated

TO MY BELOVED BROTHER ELNATHAN,

WHO WAS LIBERATED FEBRUARY 8, 1897, AND IS NOW WAITING

AND WATCHING FOR ME ON THE OTHER SIDE

OF THE SHINING RIVER.

.

CONTENTS.

———

INTRODUCTION.

This little book is called for several reasons "A Happy Year."

The author has always lived a very busy life since entering on womanhood, as a teacher for thirty-three years, and later as a lecturer and writer. The lecturing days are now ended, owing to the waning of physical vigor; and owing to impaired vision, her literary work during the past year has been limited to the answering of letters, the preparation of these weekly letters for THE BANNER OF LIGHT, and an occasional article for THE PROGRESSIVE THINKER. This comparative rest and seclusion have been grateful indeed to one who has labored so long in the busy walks of life.

But this is not the only reason that this has been a happy year. There are two others, both weightier than the one just cited.

In 1860, a dearly loved brother suffered a sun-stroke, and after distress that it is hoped is now forgotten in the happy spirit world, he suffered incarceration in an Insane Hospital for thirty-two years, until in February, 1896, she was allowed to take him to her own rooms, to spend one year in a *home*, cared for by the one who never forsook, and who loved him more than any other mortal could do. His well-nigh crushed spirit revived under the ministerations of tender care and watchful love, and in February, 1897, he was liberated from his suffering body, and passed to the arms of his father and mother, of whose care he had been deprived since 1845.

By this joyful event, the almost lifelong distress of his sister over his manifold and deepening woes for thirty-seven years was brought to an end, and her life was no longer saddened by the thought of the dreadful cloud that came so early over his pure and sensitive spirit. Reader, has not the author reason to rejoice with an unending and grateful joy! Instead of the gloom. and confinement of hospital life, he now dwells in immortal spheres. Instead of the companionship of sufferers like himself, ever pacing with unutterable pain at the heart, like the doomed in the Hall of Eblis so vividly delineated in " Vathek," he has the companionship of sweet, bright spirits—father, mother, brothers, sisters, and the vanished friends of youth—

> " Who sing, and singing in their glory move,
> And wipe the tears forever from his eyes."

The third special reason why this year has been a happy one, is that after the partial blindness of 1897, the extraction of the cataractous lenses from both eyes followed in each case by the secondary operation, she was at the beginning of this happy year fitted with glasses that give her excellent vision with one of her eyes. Owing to a series of unfortunate circumstances, the other eye does not serve her for reading, and is the source of much pain. Still, the power to read, write, and sew, for short periods of time, is a glad condition compared with being unable to read at all for several months, and the constant dread of becoming totally blind, after art should do her best.

Three reasons why this year may be called a happy one have been defined, but there are many more. One of the greatest of these is the love and sympathy expressed by countless well-wishers in nearly every State and Territory in the Union, from Canada and Mexico and from countries beyond the deep-sounding Atlantic. Her love and thanks go to each and all.

The date appended to each letter denotes the day on which it was written. They usually appeared in the BANNER OF LIGHT about thirteen days later. The first appeared in that high-toned and valuable paper, January 22, 1898; and the fifty-second, January 14, 1899.

The underlying and all-pervasive reason for happiness has not yet been expressed. The author has had that for eleven years—the fact that Spiritualism is true. Without that, this world were a desert, death a terror, and life beyond all uncertain. With that, blindness were endurable, this life a joyful journey, death, natural and beautiful, and the Beyond tinted with the rosy hues of early morning, to melt into the transcendant glory of eternity's perfect day.

Your friend,

ABBY A. JUDSON.

ARLINGTON, N. J., Dec. 19, 1898.

MISS JUDSON'S BOOKS.

"WHY SHE BECAME A' SPIRITUALIST."
  In cloth, 264 pages, $1.00.

"A HAPPY YEAR : OR, FIFTY-TWO LETTERS TO THE BANNER OF LIGHT."
  In leatherette binding, scarlet and gold, 178 pages. One copy 75 cents; five copies, to one address, $3.00.

"FROM NIGHT TO MORN ; OR AN APPEAL TO THE BAPTIST CHURCH."
  Pamphlet, 32 pages, 15 cents, ten copies for $1.00.

"THE BRIDGE BETWEEN TWO WORLDS."
  217 pages. In cloth, $1.00; paper covers, 75 cents.

Each of the above contains a portrait of the author.

"DEVELOPMENT OF MEDIUMSHIP BY TERRESTRIAL MAGNETISM."
  In cloth. 28 pages, 50 cents.

These books can be obtained by applying to ABBY A. JUDSON, Arlington, N. J.

Remit by P. O. Order or Express Order. Not in stamps.

Miss Judson's general address is Arlington, N. J., her letters being forwarded from there, wherever she may be.

"WHY SHE BECAME A SPIRITUALIST" contains twelve lectures and embodies a clear exposition of the teachings of Spiritualism. It has had a wide sale, and is conceded to be a standard work on the subject.

"FROM NIGHT TO MORN" is just the thing to put in the hands of church members, and of all inquirers. It does not antagonize; it wins, and is doing an immense work in removing prejudice.

"THE BRIDGE BETWEEN TWO WORLDS" is a book on development, and embodies all that is in "Development of Mediumship by Terrestrial Magnetism," with a great amount of additional matter. Its dedication is as follows: "This book is dedicated to all earnest souls, who desire, by harmonizing their physical bodies with universal nature, and their souls with the higher intelligences, to thus come into closer connection with the purer realms of the spirit world." It is made up of practical precepts and pure philosophy, and will assist all who read it to acquire a higher physical, mental and spiritual culture.

"A HAPPY YEAR" is the last published of Miss Judson's works.

LETTER ONE.

Insanity Ameliorated by Spiritualism.

January 9, 1898.

To the Editor of The Banner of Light:

My brother Elnathan had a sunstroke in 1860, followed by brain fever; was sent to an insane hospital in 1864, and remained under the charge of "experts" on insanity until 1896. I could never forsake him, and, though his condition was such that seeing him gave me great pain, I visited him from time to time and sent him gifts on his birthdays and at Christmas. I clung ever to the hope of being with him in his last hours.

In December, 1892, I was visiting in Bloomington, Ill., where I met Amanda M. Thayer, whose mediumship has been largely instrumental in building up Spiritualism in that section. Lingering with her one day at the dinner table she saw our old family physician, Dr. Timothy Gordon, of Plymouth, Mass., under whose supervision arrangements were made to send my brother originally to an insane hospital. Fully recognizing his identity, by Miss Thayer's vivid description, I asked him how long my brother would live. He said about four years, and he thought well of my going East to be near him. My brother's transition took place in four years and six weeks from that time.

I came East in October, 1894, and from that date till I took him home in February, 1896, I visited him seventy-one times, carrying him loving gifts and teaching him Spiritualism. Gradually I began to "see the light of thought come playing softly over lip and brow."

One of the doctors asked me what I did to my brother to make him so much better.

In my visits to my brother I said over and over to him, as to a little child, that our mother was with him often, that she loved him dearly, that his soul was the same as ever, though men judged him insane; that he would be exquisitely happy when freed from his diseased body, and that my loving thoughts were with him wherever I went. He began to realize his mother's presence, for he was a sensitive, and much in his conduct that was called insanity was due to being obsessed by dark spirits.

When his left side became partially paralyzed I was allowed to take him home. Then came the tug of war, for the dark spirits who had held him so long came the very first evening, and dreadful oaths and frightful obscene words came from lips that never before spoke wrongly in my presence. Dismayed to my heart's core, I engaged the aid of a male nurse, who stayed nine weeks, and then left for other work. He was succeeded by one who came well recommended for hospital work, whom I discharged in six weeks for unkindness to my brother. After discharging him, I made no more engagements to lecture, and from June 17, 1896, till his transition, February 8, 1897, I took entire charge of him, day and night, alone.

The first few months were dreadful. Alone in the house with him, as his screams forbade other inmates, I fought the battle with those dark, revengeful, or despairing spirits; and at last, through spirit aid, and spirit aid alone, I conquered. Our father and our mother stood by me, and the spells of obsession became less frequent and less violent. Learning what lines of thought opened the door to the low spirits, I taught my brother how to think and how to use his will against them. My will, reinforced by his own, made the last four months of his earth-life so calm and sweet that we moved into the house of friends. Though Seventh Day Adventists, with views almost antipodal to mine in many respects, their patience and their sympathy cheered us both.

His bright intellect, his loving spirit, and his fortitude
in pain, made him again what he was in youth, perhaps
the finest character I have known. Some loves of earth
fade away in the clear light of the spirit-world. Not so
with my love for him, and I can say, with the old German ballad:

> " Him loved I ever, him love I to-day:
> And him will I love forever and aye."

He comes but little to the earth-plane, where he suffered so long, and is then carefully guarded, as it is still
unsafe for him; but when I am alone he sometimes
shows me the clear light of the form and the color
which marks his identity, and I always know that he
loves me, and that he is happy.

Had Spiritualism done only this for me, restoring my
brother to sanity, that were enough. But it has done
everything for me.

> " It is my guide, my light, my all;
> It bade my dark forebodings cease:
> And through the storm and danger's thrall
> Has led me to the port of peace."

Yours for humanity and for spirituality.

LETTER TWO.

Oculists and Opticians.

January 16, 1898.

To the Editor of THE BANNER OF LIGHT:

I am happy to be able to state that the two operations performed on my right eye in New York City, have resulted in perfect success, and that the operation performed on the left eye has improved its vision to some extent. All the true sciences unfold to us the undeviating character of the laws of the universe, and happy are we who live in an age when these laws are better understood than ever before.

When the opaque lens has been removed, if there is no other trouble with the eye, colors look clearer and more beautiful than before. It was so in my own case. When the impeding lens of the right eye was removed, on the 11th of last November, I exclaimed at the clear blue of the sky. But, though the parts of the eye are clear, the removal of the lens affects the refracting power of the humors ,and this is corrected by artificial lenses in the spectacles.

To obtain the best result, this New York surgeon likes to divide the remaining back casing of the lens a number of weeks after the removal of the lens itself. By two dainty cross-cuts this filmy capsule is divided into four parts, which roll back, leaving a perfectly free access to the rays of light. This is called the secondary operation, and this is what he has done to the unfortunate left eye, which was operated on elsewhere last May.

In May, 1897, the tiny wound broke open on the third day; and being allowed to heal without interference, the result was a cystoid scar, which adheres to the iris

and impedes its natural function, which is to contract
or dilate freely in looking at different objects.

I have been thus particular, for I now come to the
sad part of my narration, and tell my sympathising
readers why it is that, though I can now see very well,
it is yet impossible to read, write or sew more than two
or three minutes at a time without an irritating pain in
the eye that was operated on last May. This cannot
now be remedied. The adhering portion of the left iris
cannot now be cut away, and I must bear this thorn in
the flesh as best I may.

How wonderful the skill by which the surgeon can
prescribe to the optician the exact form of the glasses
to be made! A variation of the tenth part of a hair's
breadth wrong, and the glass is wrong. And yet far
more skill is employed by Nature in many billions of
human eyes now used on the earth plane, to say nothing of the eyes of all the animals. And no human skill
has ever made an optical instrument equal to the human
eye. The utmost man can do is to follow Nature.
"Art can *obey*, but not *surpass*."

As finite beings, what can we know of God, or Infinite Intelligence? Only by its manifestations in universal law. No more can we ever know than this. To
this law do we bow. To this law do we endeavor to
conform. When deviating from this law causes pain,
to this pain do we submit. Better to suffer pain from
violated law than live in a lawless universe.

I am thankful to see again, to walk again with my
fellows, seeing like them. But, were it mine to choose,
better physical blindness than spiritual blindness! In
a subsequent letter I hope to be permitted to tell some
of the spiritual sights, some of the angelic ministrations,
that soothed my pain, and, in spite of bandaged eyes,
brought some of heaven before my inner vision.

Yours for humanity and for spirituality.

LETTER THREE.

How my Father, Adoniram Judson, who passed to the Spirit side of Life in 1850, saved my Eye.

January 23, 1898.

To the Editor of The Banner of Light:

It has been remarked that if there were no eyes to see, light would not exist; if there were no ears to hear, then no sound; in other words, light and sound are only effects of vibration on certain nerves of the body. While this may be true, it is impossible for us not to accept the testimony of our own senses; and on this testimony we believe that the sun, stars, sentient beings on the earth-plane, flowers, music. and human voices do exist. They exist to you and me because we see and hear tokens on which we found our belief. It is not the eye that sees, it is not the ear that hears, it is the soul within, the real being that uses these organs in order thus to know of a physical universe.

In like manner, the soul within, the real being, believes in the existence of a spiritual universe, because phenomena are presented to the inner eye and the inner ear that are the tokens of its existence. If these tokens are accepted as evidence regarding the material universe, it is surely fair to accept them in regard to the spiritual universe. To be sure, they are only phenomena in either case. As such, they give us belief, but not knowledge. When it comes to really knowing, the only thing that a finite being can really know is his own mental existence. "I think, therefore I am."

The philosophic and high-minded editor of *The Monist* says that all beings who have ever existed, exist within each one of us; and when you see your deceased father, it is because he is momentarily projected from your own interior being. That is the *Monist* way of looking at it. The Spiritualist way is quite different. The Spiritualist says: "I see my deceased father, because he really exists individually outside of me; and I see him by using the eyes of my spiritual body, which can sense the vibrations of the more ethereal mode of existence which is his, since he passed out of his fleshly body." That is the way in which I regard these spiritual phenomena. They prove to me that spiritual beings exist, just as seeing a man go by the house proves to me that he exists, and that he did go by the house.

Last November, when I lay in the hospital with both eyes closely bandaged, and wondering what would be the result of the operation, I saw my father come in at the door. His face looked anxious, but as I thus realized that he was there to help me, a great wave of encouragement rolled over my soul.

The great danger after the removal of a cataractous lens is lest the patients tear off the bandages, to relieve the itching and the irksomeness caused by lying flat so long. Unruly patients sometimes do this, and the best intentioned patient might do it when asleep. Rubbing the eye would break open the tiny wound, and perhaps make the operation ineffectual forever.

On the eighth night after the lens was removed, I had a terrifying dream. A dead girl *would* get up and walk close to my side, upstairs, downstairs, and everywhere. I screamed for aid, but none came, for all were terrified and had fled. The fright awoke me, and I found that my right hand had pushed aside the mask and the bandages, and was just at the partly healed eye. I replaced the bandages and mask, and put my hand under the bedclothes.

I lay wondering why I should have so dreadful a dream. Suddenly I realized that the dream woke me and saved my eye. Some good spirit, I thought, took that means of arousing me. Instantly there stood my father, his face not anxious this time, but calm, glorified, triumphant. It may be that some undeveloped spirit got control of my hand, and thought to prevent my future usefulness by ruining the wounded eye. Paul says truly: "We wrestle not against flesh and blood, but against principalities, against powers, against *spiritual* wickedness in high places." But I had no fear after that, for I knew that my father would be a match for them.

Yours for humanity and for spirituality.

LETTER FOUR.

My Mother's Spirit Light.

January 30, 1898.

To the Editor of THE BANNER OF LIGHT:

It seems to be one of the laws of spiritual progression that while the higher can come to the lower, in order to assist those who are seeking to rise, yet the lower can ascend only as they become fitted to do so. Spirits of unusual brightness have been through the lower grades of the great school, to which they can return at will; but those of the lower benches must go on step by step, and their progression will be the more rapid as they try to assist those who are still less advanced than they.

Most of those who pass out of the body linger for awhile near the earth-plane, and are easily seen in their spirit form by the clairvoyant. As their development advances their forms become more ethereal, though they always retain a likeness to the former fleshly body. As they advance to higher conditions, though they are just as recognizable by those whose home is on their plane, the form is not seen by the ordinary clairvoyant, but they appear as lights to him, though the soul can always at will assume a grosser spirit form than can be seen by spiritual eyes on or near the earth-plane.

Dante, though his "Inferno" is wofully marred by the horrible views taught in the thirteenth century, yet unfolds many spiritual truths in his "Paradiso." Taken by his arisen guide, Beatrice, to the upper realms, he sees such spirits as St. John and Thomas Aquinas only as lights, though they, of course, knew each other by their forms. And these different characteristic lights he learned to recognize.

All this tallies with my own experience as a clairvoyant. When my spiritual vision began, nine years ago, I saw my father, whose transition took place in 1850, many, many times. As time passed on, I saw him less and less, and have scarcely seen him of late, except the two occasions at the hospital, as described in my last letter, when he took the old earth appearance to cheer and strengthen me. Meanwhile, his spiritual influence on me has increased, and is distinctly recognized. Already the promise he made to me in 1890, through the slate writing of Sarah De Wolf, is in process of fulfillment: "Soul to soul, like the blending of light, will our souls mingle." A missionary while here, he is still a missionary. His powerful will carries him everywhere, and he can avail himself of varied means to make himself felt in Burmah, in America, with his children, and with the clergy.

My mother, who passed on in 1845, even then a finely-attuned spirit, comes but little to the earth-plane, except by influence. I have seen her form distinctly but once, and that was some eight years ago. For six years I have often seen her light, and I know it at once. The first time, in 1892, being in both mental and physical trouble, I begged her to come. A large, oval, purple light, deep in the centre and shading off by imperceptible gradations, came from the left, and gently swept my face. She replied to my words by many eager little raps, *within* my organism. I love to see that purple light. It caresses me; it blesses me. It takes away every kind of pain. When I see this light I feel that it is more closely my mother than if she put on an earthly form. It is my mother's glorified form, and it looks to me here like a purple light. Three times she tried to materialize through mediums, but after I came home the last time, I said, "Don't try again, dearest mother; there is no need. I know you come. Why should you put on an outside form which is, after all, not really *you*, for me to feel with my fleshly hands?"

My father wrote me last spring through an unknown psychic, "The soul needs no tongue, my child." How true! I did not need the gentle reminder. He wrote it for those around, who desired to see what would be written for me.

But my space is used up, and I will only add that my left eye is less painful, and we hope that its poor little iris will learn to adjust itself to its imprisoned state.

Yours for humanity and for spirituality.

LETTER FIVE.

"Enny."

February 6, 1898.

To the Editor of THE BANNER OF LIGHT :

Usually I know the subject of my letter a day or two before writing. Not so this time. Various themes occurred to me, but none was right till, just as I was ready to sit down to my always pleasant task, I knew. The object of this letter is to show the power of love to restore a disordered spirit.

One year ago my brother lay dying. His happy soul was freed on February 8. He was known here by strangers as Elnathan Judson; to his intimates and in the family, as El; but his baby name in Burmah was Enny. The name of Enny had been long disused, and well nigh forgotten. The summer before his transition he told me that our father and mother had been talking to him. Questions elicited the fact that he did not see them, nor recognize their voices, but *knew* it was they, and that they said to him: "Papa and mamma love Enny dearly." The use of the baby name proved to me that they had indeed been with him.

An aged Burmese couple, Ko Boke and Mah Boke, had loved us dearly in Burmah. I well remember that the good old woman was at the jetty to bid us farewell, with our favorite cakes, and how she lifted up her voice and wailed as she went up from the boat. I saw her in Wichita, Kan., when in illness and depression. She had been rubbing my feet. Old Ko Boke attended my brother closely in his illness, and if I found it necessary to do anything he did not like, he said Ko Boke did not like it.

Once when visiting my brother at the hospital, and talking to him of mother, he said he remembered well how she looked once at dusk, standing at the end of the veranda, in a light dress, with her light brown hair, looking at him. I said to him: "Yes, my darling; and by-and-by, when you are in spirit-land, mother will be standing on the veranda of her beautiful house. She will see you coming, and she will hasten down the steps and fold her arms about her dear little son, and she will lead you up into the house, to live with her in her lovely home." A sweet smile came into his face.

Those who had known my parents intimately said this brother had our father's broad laugh, but his smile was like that of our mother. Bless their dear hearts! They are all together now. "When shall I their chorus join?" The tears come. They say: "Not yet, daughter. We still have work for you to do."

About ten weeks before his transition, the knee of the paralyzed side drew spasmodically up opposite his chest. It gave him great pain, and I summoned a physician. He said it often occurred, and could not be helped. After he had left the body, this doctor asked if the cords had to be cut to put him into the coffin. But my father knew what to do, and impressed me in the night how to arrange a pad around the ankle, and tapes, and a flat-iron to hang over the foot of the bed. The device drew the limb so gradually that it gave him no pain, was a perfect success, and we used it till it became unnecessary.

After I made use of this device his confidence in me was unbounded. If I proposed anything, his invariable answer was: "You know best;" or "Do as you think best, dear."

I was alone with him the last five hours, and every time I asked him if he was in pain he always said, "No pain, but it is difficult to swallow." Once I said, "Will you forgive me, darling, for every sign of impatience?" "Yes, yes," he said; and then lifting his dear, dim eyes to my face, he said: "You are very dear to me, my sister." Many times while he drew those labored breaths I said: "Abby does love Enny *so much.*"

Our parents bore him away at once, when he ceased to breathe, and he did not return to earth for nine days. Then he came to me. I saw his dear face.

The funeral services were when I was alone with his form, before the undertaker came with the hearse. I was re-arranging the flowers, when an influence took me, and with joyful tears and hands raised to heaven I summoned all who loved us, and committed his precious soul to their tender, watchful care forevermore, in the name of the Infinite Love of the universe. He was not there, of course. The others came. "All we love and all who love us." Oh! how thankful I am daily that he could be with me for one year, and that I could in

some measure atone for those terrible and doleful
thirty-two years in insane hospitals.

Yours for humanity and for spirituality.

LETTER SIX.

Spirit aid before the Extraction of the Cataract.

February 13, 1898.

To the Editor of THE BANNER OF LIGHT :

I would like to tell you how Spiritualism aided me
before and during the critical operation to which I have
been subjected. It is useless to deny it; one cannot
but dread—especially when having once undergone the
same and suffered at the extraction of the lens—in spite
of the cocaine so freely applied. The eye is, as we all
know, exquisitely sensitive, and no doubt the higher
development which we so gladly seek renders us more
sensitive.

I have heard of a little boy who was pitied because
he had stubbed his toe. "*I'm* not hurt," said he, with
all the advanced thought of a *fin du siècle* boy. "My
little shell of a body may be hurt, but I'm not hurt."
A good ministerial brother who visited me afterwards
at the hospital, adverted to this incident, and we laugh-
ingly concluded that the interior of the eye seems, to
say the least, nearer the centre of being than an outside shell.

Well, having made all arrangements, I placed myself
in bed, for a week's sojourn therein, some two or three
hours before the arrival of the surgeon—"head inquis-
itorial functionary," as I sometimes called him—the
sub-doctors, in solemn row, being his "familiars."
Some may wonder why I prepared so long beforehand.

I was guided to do so, as is the case with many of my acts in life, for the way was thus opened for spiritual manifestations that strengthened me for what was to come.

There were three who manifested themselves—my father, my mother, and my lately-arisen brother. My mother's light was almost constant for two or three hours, and I wish that I could describe the heavenly beauty of the manifestation. Just above me in front she brooded over her child, pouring down floods of magnetism. Purple being still her color, there were the most exquisite clouds of soft, pinkish purple, that formed themselves constantly into a large whirl. This whirl was not in stupendous action, as when mighty spirits conjoin to build a world, as alluded to on page 128 of "The Bridge Between Two Worlds." This whirl, constantly forming, dissolving and re-forming, was my mother, existent rather than active, and existing to bless. When left alone for a few moments I talked with her, and she breathed upon me a mother's love.

Sometimes she gave way to my father. Years ago his color was red, indicating force. Now he comes in a great, powerful white light, full of purity, courage, and high resolve. He thus let me know that he was close at hand. Then this would disappear, and mother would resume her tender watch. And once, only once, just before the surgeon came, I saw a little upright pillar of deep blue. It brightened, till it was a soft, light and living blue, and I knew that my brother, who one year before was suffering on the earth-plane, had now come to bring sweet comfort to the sister who always loved him, and will love him forever. He now dwells with mother in higher spheres, developing his immortal powers; and in ages to come he will be a powerful influence to uplift multitudes, especially those who suffer in the same way that he suffered so long.

The aid granted was so effectual that all those present said the removal of the lens was rarely performed on so tranquil and quiet a subject. They expressed their surprise, for they knew that I was nervous, and not over strong. I told those sweet nurses much before I left the hospital. People cannot know me very long without knowing that I am a Spiritualist.

Yours for humanity and for spirituality.

LETTER SEVEN.

Mr. J. O. Barrett and "The Medium of the Rockies."

February 20, 1898.

To the Editor of THE BANNER OF LIGHT:

Your issue of February 19th bears upon its title page, "In Memoriam: Joseph Osgood Barrett," and an almost speaking portrait of his careworn and benign face. My first thought was, "Bless him! He is now an angel, but only because he had begun to be an angel while in the fleshly body."

Well do I remember meeting Mr. Barrett in Minneapolis in 1888, and the kind trouble he took to come to see me at my rooms, and the wisdom shown in his words and in his subsequent letters, warning me of certain pitfalls which my enthusiastic acceptance of Spiritualism had laid for my inexperienced feet. He was in line with my father's later caution, "Use your own judgment; let reason balance the manifestations."

Mr. Barrett was the first Spiritualist of eminence, culture and breeding that I had met, for this was before Bishop A. Beals had come to St. Paul, and two years before I attended my first camp meeting. I was just a tyro, and attended séances with other investigators. I did not accept Spiritualism, dear friends, because of the learning and culture that I found at that time; I ac-

cepted it because it was true. And Mr. Barrett, who
possessed all the qualities that make men esteemed by
the best men and women, showed me a purity, a wisdom, and a courage that I have never seen excelled. I
was also struck by his tender devotion to his delicate
wife, the wife of his youth. My heart bleeds for her in
her present grief. Yet a little while, and those who
love him will rejoin him in a fairer clime than this.

> "Farewell, good man, good angel now. This hand
> Soon, like thine own, shall lose its cunning too;
> Soon shall this soul, like thine, bewildered stand,
> Then leap to thread the free, unfathomed blue."

I had hoped to meet him again here, but our meeting
is now postponed to a brighter day, I believe, Mr.
Editor, that you derive some of your noble qualities
from the brother of your own father—J. O. Barrett.

The first book that I read after recovering my sight
was kindly sent to me by Mr. Newman, of the *Philosophical Journal*, and is entitled "John Brown, the
Medium of the Rockies." It is a good book to read,
and to lend to those who will not or cannot buy. No
one can read the simple, unvarnished account of how
Mopoloquist prophesied, healed and instructed through
him, without feeling that it is all true. And truth,
pure, unadulterated truth, is what the world craves
from every writer, medium and speaker. No genius,
no inspiration, no learning, no eloquence, no mediumistic power, is worth anything if truth be not there.

John Brown did not seek to be a medium. The
spirits found him a fit instrument, and they sought him.
And if there were any indications that some one tried
to misuse what came through him, they withdrew the
power. I will relate an instance, ending on Page 51.

Mopoloquist often unrolled before him, when asleep,
what would happen the next day. The pioneers, his
companions, did everything possible to prevent the ac-
complishment of the prophecy. But invariably, when

the hour drew near, they all forgot it, and every word and act came out exactly as prophesied. So they learned to watch eagerly for his waking, in order to learn what was to happen.

At last one of them, named Timothy Goodale, proposed to John Brown to tell him alone what was to take place, and he would divide with him what he would win from the others. Brown refused, and resented the offer. The next time, Mopoloquist told Brown to have nothing to do with Goodale. The next night he looked sad, and taking off his hat, took the manuscript from it, but could not unroll it. The next night he was sad and silent, and could not even take off his hat. The next night he stood in silence, and went away with sorrow and regret. Since then he has visited Brown only at long intervals, "being apparently under the restraint of some one superior to himself."

Do any of my readers know of a man named John Brown who is bad? I know of three, and they are all good men and true. There was Dr. John Brown of Edinboro', who wrote "Rab and His Friends," and other works, showing a refined nature and humane heart; there was John Brown of Harper's Ferry, the old hero, "who made the gallows holy when he perished by the cord;" and here is this noble "Medium of the Rockies," still living in California, and revered by all who know him. The value of the book is enhanced by the admirable introduction by Prof. J. S. Loveland.

Yours for humanity and for spirituality.

LETTER EIGHT.

The "Filth and Fraud" Accusation.

February 27, 1898.

To the Editor of THE BANNER OF LIGHT:

I have an experience to relate which is, alas! but too
common to all Spiritualists who come in contact with
the church.

There is a church in New York called the Adoniram
Judson Memorial Church. The humane labors connected with it go much further than with ordinary
churches. There are the fresh air home for children in
the country, the Orphans' Home adjoining the church,
the dispensary where the poor are treated without
charge, the kindergarten, the free ice water in summer,
and many other similar adjuncts to his work of love.
The words of the preacher have great weight, because
his life is well known to be in accord with the kindness
he preaches.

Circumstances had prevented me from ever attending
the services at this memorial church, for when in New
York for a Sunday I was either speaking myself, or confined in the hospital. But the first Sunday of the new
year, remembering the kind visit of the preacher to me
when ill, I was glad to feel well enough to go over from
Arlington to attend his church. The text was: "Take
heed that ye despise none of these little ones, for in
heaven their angels do always behold the face of our
Father in heaven." It was a beautiful sermon, and
tenderly did he inculcate our duty, not only to children,
but to all who are incapacitated in any way from standing on a par with their fellows. When he came to the
reason assigned, he said he thought only Jesus could
have thought of such a reason—that their angels behold
God's face. A worldly man might say we had better

be good to little ones because by and by we shall be old
and they will be strong, and can injure us. He then
went on to say that though many of his hearers would
not agree with him, he upheld the literal truth of the
text, because, said he, everybody has a guardian angel.
"You may not like this notion," he said, "because you
revolt from the saint-worship of the Roman Catholic
church, and because you are disgusted with the fraud
and the filth of Spiritualism."

These words gave me great pain. In my father's
Memorial Church, and I sitting there! Later, I took
occasion to write to the preacher that it was just as un-
reasonable to characterize Spiritualism as filthy and
fraudful, as to say that Christianity is treacherous and
murderous, because Judas and Guiteau professed to
be followers of Christ.

But Christian ministers (except the most ignorant
among them) are not opposed to Spiritualism on account
of filth and fraud. They well know that the bravest,
truest and most enlightened persons in the community
have found out that Spiritualism is true. That is not
their real reason for opposing it, though they proclaim
this as the reason, in order to impose on the ignorant,
and in order to daunt those who hear them who are in-
vestigating it.

The real reason why ministers and church leaders
hate Spiritualism is because they are afraid of it. They
know perfectly well that they cannot control the thinking of those who have found out that decarnate spirits
can inspire American mediums in this decade, just as
truly as decarnate spirits used to inspire Jews two
thousand to four thousand years ago; and it is ten to
one that these modern spirits are broader, more scientific, and quite as spiritual as those of long ago.

They abhor Spiritualism because they cannot pen us up
by the words of the Hebrew Bible, and are losing their
power to rule the minds of men. They will use every
means to retain this power, and the contest will be long
and hard.

As to fraud and filth, we know well enough that they characterize some of the hangers-on, and some mediums who are controlled by vicious spirits; but this will diminish, and surely it cannot be deprecated by our church friends nearly so much as by the great mass of Spiritualists.

There is a very simple way to exclude all filth and fraud from spiritual manifestations; a way that I have practiced for several years; but as I have already used up the space accorded to me in your valuable columns, I will, with your permission, Mr. Editor, give an account of this effectual method in a subsequent letter.

Yours for humanity and for spirituality.

LETTER NINE.

Moral Purity essential to good Mediumship.

March 6, 1898.

To the Editor of THE BANNER OF LIGHT:

It gives a true lover of Spiritualism great pain to hear this constant cry of fraud by its opponents; and when to the disgraceful word of fraud is added the still more opprobrious term of filth, it requires some nerve to still say unflinchingly in the face of those who revile the name, "Yes, I am a Spiritualist."

We who have already begun to drink of the pure water flowing down to us from celestial regions, who have found in spirit communion strength for our daily needs, and who anticipate the dissolution of the fleshly body with joy unspeakable and full of glory, are not dismayed by these epithets, flung out by those who are either ignorant of Spiritualism, or, knowing something of its value, yet dread what will inevitably cause " the

surrender of Orthodoxy." But many seekers are not
as far along, and we should by all means take steps to
render such accusations impossible, or their falsity
apparent to the most cursory glance. Besides, possessing as we do the truth that can alone uplift
mankind and prepare it for the heaven beyond by making a heaven of the life here, we owe it to our own self
respect to quickly and wisely present our views in a
way to win the confidence and the esteem of the world
at large.

One of the most pernicious doctrines that has ever
been sustained by Spiritualists is that the moral character of the medium is of no consequence. I have
heard that constantly sustained by Spiritualists of long
standing during the last ten years, and I never heard
it without dissenting from it in my own soul; and
many have thrown stumbling-blocks in my way in many
places because I have contended, both in speaking and
in writing, for making a pure, moral character more
important than mediumship. This view is fully brought
out in chapters 3, 4, 5 and 18 of "The Bridge Between
Two Worlds," written in 1894, and it is in fact the
keynote to the whole work. My angelic helpers earnestly desire that mediums in general should read and
act upon their teachings as given there. But alas!
many mediums dread these doctrines because their
adoption would anger their controls, and cause their
withdrawal and the consequent withdrawal of the
money these controls help them to make. If such
mediums would make the development of their own
souls their first object, this effort would at once open
the door to a high order of spirits; and, as they have
real mediumistic power, this power would be utilized
by these new controls, and they would find a beauty
and a glory in their work that is beyond their present
power to conceive. But as long as many believers per-
sist in the claim that character is of no consequence to
a medium, we cannot be surprised that many sensi-

tives, whose susceptibility to spirit control proves certain yielding strands in their mental make-up, should say the same, to the great delight of certain low spirits who believe it, too, and are glad to retain the power they have so long held.

Alas! my space is nearly all gone, and I have but just begun. How shall we, who are not acting mediums, aid to develop a pure mediumship, and thus conquer the accusations of filth and fraud? In the first place let us seek communications only from high and noble spirits, whose teachings can ennoble and purify our own characters, opening the door to undeveloped spirits only with a view to aiding them by our own moral strength. And, in the second place, let us have no private sittings, attend no séances, and patronize no public test mediums unless we are sure that these mediums make their own personal purity and truth their first object in life, thus making it possible for exalted spirits to *worthily* communicate with mortals through them. We have many such mediums in our ranks, and only such should be patronized, both in public and in private. A different sort of medium should be discountenanced, and this is especially necessary because one with a low control (because he does not insist on a higher one) can readily amuse a crowd of outsiders and fun-seekers in a way that a person of high aspirations and refined manners cannot do.

Yours for humanity and for spirituality.

LETTER TEN.

Motives for Seeking Mediumship.

March 13, 1898.

To the Editor of THE BANNER OF LIGHT :

I am in frequent receipt of letters from persons who desire to become mediums, and ask my assistance to that end. A late one was from a settled pastor of a church, who wishes to speak under inspiration. Another was from a person who wants mediumship in order to make money, and who offered me a large per cent. of her first winnings if I would aid her to this method of making a handsome living.

To the minister I wrote a letter full of caution, reminding him of the countless numbers of undeveloped spirits close to the earth plane; but, if his leading motive was to get an inspiration to help to uplift and spiritualize mankind, I bade him God-speed. Later he sent for " The Bridge Between Two Worlds," and with the aid of "good, pure, true, loving, wise and strong spirits," he will doubtless do great good in his day and generation.

As to the other seeker for mediumship, I advised her to let it alone, because her motive in acquiring it seemed to be such as would open the door of her inner being to a dangerous class of spirits. I asked her to try to make money in some other way, and meanwhile to try to develop her soul to beauty, truth, and goodness, by her every word, thought and action. Later, when her aims had become highly aspirational, if she had mediumistic power, noble spirits would adopt her for their own, and she would be a medium between earth and heaven for good spirits not only here, but after she had left the fleshly body. I did not hear from this dear soul again. May highest heaven aid her, and

every one who aspires to be the mouthpiece of the
angel world!

Mediumship is the most sacred gift that has ever
been given to mortals. The Nazarene, if the story be
true, felt it to be so. When a powerful decarnate spirit
sought to take control of him by using his gifts to
worldly uses, he combated him. This spirit told him
to appease his hunger by turning stones into bread,
bade him tempt angel aid by leaping from the topmost
spire of the temple, and capped the climax by telling
him he would make him ruler of the known world if he
would acknowledge his mastership by bowing down
and worshiping him.

To these impure suggestions the gifted Nazarene
turned a deaf ear, and resolved then and there to use
his rare powers to relieve human suffering and to aid
to spiritualize the race. Those who have read "Why
She Became a Spiritualist," may remember that this
subject is quite fully treated in the chapter entitled,
"The Spiritualism of Jesus." That, and the preceding
one, entitled, "What Jesus really Taught," were writ-
en in Minneapolis in 1891, under the inspiration of
Henry Ward Beecher, though the writer did not dream
at that time that she was a medium of any phase.

Whether the account of Jesus be historically true or
not, does not matter. It is no less a sublime lesson for
the guidance of every incarnate soul in the nineteenth
century who aspires to be a medium between souls in
the physical and the more purely spiritual world, between this shadow life and the real and vivid life on
the other side of the thin veil.

Yours for humanity and for spirituality.

LETTER ELEVEN.

Home Treatment for the Insane.

March 20, 1898.

To the Editor of The Banner of Light:

As some persons having friends whose intellects are disordered have written to me inquiring for more particulars regarding the work done for my brother through me by good decarnate spirits, so that they may profit by my experience, I feel impelled to make this work the subject of the present letter.

Those who care for insane persons, as for other sick people, should, so far as possible, be near of kin, and those who love them truly and deeply. Only such could have the patience requisite for a work like this. If outsiders are employed, as some cases would require, they should be under the close and personal supervision of those who love the patient the most dearly. It is injurious, though sometimes necessary, for the patient to be shut up with those similarly afflicted. Mental disease, like some physical diseases, is catching. And we who are enlightened by Spiritualism shudder to think of the thousands of undeveloped and malign spirits who brood over insane hospitals, and combine to "make the last state of that man even worse than the first."

Some of the best hospitals in Europe place the patients separately, one insane person being boarded in a wholly sane family. This is admirable, when practicable, and we hope this method will become more prevalent in the United States.

When persons are dangerously and violently insane, they can be placed in a padded room at home, or fastened to a bedstead by long, smooth straps around the wrists and ankles, which give ample play to the limbs, and yet prevent the sufferer from injuring others or himself. It should be remembered that some who were gentle on first going to a hospital, become violently insane and dangerous, because they find that they cannot get away, cannot see those they love, and come to feel that they have deserted them. This was the case with my poor brother.

Before confinement, and yet insane, he spent his time in writing poems and essays on purity, and in taking long walks. For awhile at the hospital he continued to write, and was buoyed up by the hope of being released when his surgeon brother had a furlough from the war. He had the furlough, visited him, and of course (though with a breaking heart) had to leave him there. Months passed on, and the gentle, scholarly recluse became, through *despair*, violently insane. This continued for over two years, and then, with conquered will, he became quiet, and sank into the condition that continued for thirty years, until I was allowed to take the poor sufferer to my home and give him the sweetness of home life for one sad year. I well know, and he has assured me of the same from the spirit side of life, that if he had been treated as I treated him, from the beginning of his diseased condition, his life would not have been a wasted and an agonized one.

I have a minute account in writing of those first months of confinement. A devoted friend went to the hospital every week or two, and wrote long letters detailing his condition, whether he saw him or not. I kept those letters, but could never bear to read them again after the first time, until the transition of my idolized brother from what was indeed "a vale of tears" for him, to the exquisite joys and reunions of the spirit-land. No, no; whatever be the disease, typhoid fever, smallpox, insanity, Bright's disease, whatever it be, keep your dear one at home, and cared for by those who love him best, *if possible*.

I know of a family of which the father became violently and incurably insane. The mother said he should

never go to a hospital. They built a room with wooden
walls four inches thick, and carefully padded. He lived
seventeen years, and though his reason was never restored on the earth-plane, yet think of the joy and gratitude of that liberated soul when he welcomes by and by
that wife and those children who ministered to him in
his sore need to his home in the spirit-land.

By the way, how beautiful it was in Fannie Allyn to
speak so tenderly and effectually to the female prison-
ers in the jail of St. Louis! My arisen brother greets
her, and thanks her through me for that noble day's
work.

Yours for humanity and for spirituality.

LETTER TWELVE.

The Golden Jubilee of Modern Spirit-ualism.

March 27, 1898

To the Editor of THE BANNER OF LIGHT:

The eyes of the Spiritualists of the world are turned
about this time to the little village of Hydesville, N. Y.,
because there a decarnate spirit "Made the *rap* heard
round the world." Taking place at a definite house,
and the date, March 31, 1848, being an established fact,
occurring near the city of Rochester, in the heart of
American civilization, and soon heralded far and wide
by the press, these well-attested signals from the spirit
side of life may well be taken as an objective point, like
Mohammed's flight from Mecca, or the alleged birth of
the Nazarene. But sometime before this date do well
attested facts bear witness that the organized forces of
the higher spirit regions had opened the door between
their realms and ours in many different places. Their
efforts were especially directed to the United States,

because in a republic whose constitution makes an impassible chasm between Church and State, there was less likelihood that civil authority would crush their efforts, as used to be done in more tyrannical and superstitious times and countries.

In 1843 high spirits had spoken and written through Andrew Jackson Davis, and had begun through him a series of memorable books. And more than ten years before that, John Brown, a lad among the Rocky Mountains, was convincing his associates, by his constantly-fulfilled prophecies, that he was the mouth-piece of decarnate spirits. Brown was born in 1817, he was seven when the high souled Mopoloquist took him for his medium, and before he was twenty he was already proving the truth of spirit-return.

John Brown's work was confined for many years to the far West, and was but little known. Davis's marvelous and inspiring communications appealed to the learned, the scientific, and the loftily spiritual; but the raps made by the murdered pedlar through the little Fox girls could be heard by everybody. Those who took the pains to make a personal investigation were forced to admit that there was "something in it;" and though the horrified and suspicious clergy said this something or somebody was Satan himself, the thing could not be hushed. "And still the wonder grew."

For the past seven years we have wondered how it was that this newly-fledged marvel received the name of Spiritualism. Who, in the name of diction, bestowed this name so singularly inappropriate to the thing signified? Had they called it Spiritism, no more, no less, the name would have been just. The raps proved the existence of spirits without a fleshly body. The poor pedlar, so foully murdered, proved himself a genuine spirit. He had no fleshly body, but he could rap out his thoughts and prove his individual intelligence.

Of Spiritualism proper, of its beauty and its glory, it seems probable that only one of the Fox girls had much conception while a dweller on the planet. We allude, of course, to the noble, self-respecting , and self-controlled Leah.

Spiritism is one thing, Spiritualism is another. The first is derived from the word spirit; the second, from the adjective spiritual. Spiritism lays the foundation; Spiritualism is the magnificent, yet never to be completed, edifice. Spiritism is the seed planted in the doubtful yet seeking heart; Spiritualism is the beautiful tree with branches ever dropping balm on imprisoned souls, and yet ever stretching and growing toward the infinite.

We thank with unspeakable joy those glorious immortals who banded together to bring the certainty of spirit-existence to earth-bound souls, and still more for the sweet fruitage and the magnificent promise of the fairest queen that ever reigned over the human intellect and the human heart—pure, ever-growing Spiritualism!

Yours for humanity and for spirituality.

LETTER THIRTEEN.

The Exteriorization of the Motor Forces in Man.

April 4, 1898.

To the Editor of The Banner of Light:

In your issue of March 12 is an article entitled "The Exteriorization of the Motor Forces of Man," which seems to me so valuable that it is worth the careful consideration of every Spiritualist. The above words are the title of a recent work by M. de Rochas. A previous work by him recorded a series of experiments proving that under certain conditions the sensibility is removed beyond the physical body, while the present one shows experimentally that the human spirit, while still embodied in fleshly form, can move objects more or less remote that are not reached by the body proper. His next work will be on "The Phantoms of the Living," and we hope that he will then carry all these premises to their legitimate conclusion, and give one to the world to be called "The Phantoms of the Dead."

Though we are delighted that so careful, truthful, and scientific a man as M. de Rochas is doing this needed and effectual work, the fact that we, still in the form, can and do move tables, produce raps, and even slate writing, without the intervention of disembodied spirits, is known to many thinking Spiritualists. In fact, how could it be otherwise? for we are to-day spirits *just as truly* as when we become disembodied. Some of us can do these things, many decarnate spirits can do them. And if we want on any occasion only disembodied spirits to do them, it is of the first, the last, and the always paramount consequence, that not only every medium, but each and every sitter as well, should when sitting become perfectly passive mentally. If one individual in the sitting allows his own opinions or his own will to be active on any of the subjects connected with the desired communications from the other side of life, then it is quite possible that his mental attitude takes control of the manifestation, and prevents the anxious disembodied friend from expressing himself through the raps, the table movements, the slate writing, or whatever phase of expression it may be.

Negative persons, with weak wills, are easily used by spirits, either in the body or out of the body; but, in our opinion, the best results are obtained in the long run through individuals who are positive by nature, but who have learned *how* to make themselves perfectly passive when they choose to do so. This subject, vitally important to all who seek to communicate with those who have left the physical body, is, of course, fully treated in "The Bridge Between Two Worlds."

In 1891, while speaking in Wisconsin, a sincere Spiritualist invited me to a sitting at his house. He had made the table himself, and he and his wife had sat at it for years and years, opposite each other at the ends. On this occasion I sat on one side, and another person opposite me. This evening the answer to every question was in accord with the positive opinion of this good, sincere Spiritualist. The answers regarding my own affairs, and those of the family where I was staying, often contradicted the truth, where the truth was unknown to him. Unconsciously to himself, he made the movements and the raps, and the disembodied friends could not express themselves. This good man had not learned to become passive when sitting at his table.

In Cincinnati, in 1894, I stepped into a jewelry store. The proprietor was a Secularist. The conversation turning upon Spiritualism, he said he could produce slate writing, and "spirits" would not do it at all. We took a clean slate, and laid it face down on the glass counter He put his hand on it, and I put my hand on it. The writing came 'in a minute. I heard the writing going on, and I read it afterward. It was on some every day topic. In this case it was written by a spirit, but probably the spirit was still embodied.

In 1895, in the East, I saw much of a woman through whom loud raps came. She would hold a folded newspaper or some large object of light weight in one hand, stretching the arm out, and answers to questions came by loud raps. At every rap her arm quivered slightly. She would not do it in the presence of persons whom she considered learned or scientific, but she did it willingly for others. She well knew that it came from herself in some way. The answer always accorded with what she thought might be the case, but were untrue as often as not. As the woman proved herself at other times untruthful, slanderous and malicious, I had no use for her gift. But the credulous thought her a wonder ul rapping medium.

These are only three instances, out of perhaps fifty, that have come under my own observation, that accord with the deductions from the investigations of M. de Rochas. These deductions are legitimate, but they do not invalidate the *bona fide* communications that come daily from disembodied spirits through honest, high-minded mediums, who understand themselves, and whose spiritual gifts and graces have enabled good spirits to reach mortals through their organisms.

Yours for humanity and for spirituality.

LETTER FOURTEEN.

My Upholstered Chair.

April 10, 1898.

To the Editor of THE BANNER OF LIGHT:

In my sequestered, quiet, and seemingly lonely life, I have time to think, especially at the evening hour. The days are crowded with work of various kinds; by lamplight there are letters to be written; but when the evening begins to gather, before I light my lamp, is the the time to sit and rest, and receive impressions from the immortal helpers. Some might think it strange, but one old chair is the dearest to me. Sitting in it in Minneapolis, I once found myself in my father's arms, and we held tender converse together. In the same chair I wrote, under a powerful impulse, the letter read in Malden, Mass., at the centennial of his birthday. While in it, came the loud raps that bespoke his nearness to me. While in the same chair, I was about to read a newspaper, when he made me rise and hasten to an inner room. My removal was followed by two loud reports. A small, improvised cannon across the street exploded, and a jagged piece of iron, one inch by five or six inches, tore through the plate-glass window, struck the opposite corner of the room, and fell in the third corner. Every object in the room was powdered with fine glass. Had I remained in my chair, I should have been frightfully injured, and perhaps killed. If I had been reading, the piece of iron would have struck my head; if leaning back, it would have torn through my jaw. This was July 4, 1889.

While sitting in this chair on Thanksgiving Day, 1888, in bright daylight, I saw my father's etherealized form. I think he was aided to make this presentation by the magnetic force proceeding from a friend, now residing, I think, in Pasadena, Cal. He had dined with me that day. About three o'clock we were each sitting by a window, facing each other. I was sleepy, and my feet were cold. I opened my eyes, but felt too sluggish to move. In the little camp-chair which I carried to Europe with me, and used in many a memorable place, sat my Grandmother Judson. I never saw her in earth life. No doubt her tremendous will force, inherited by her missionary son, aided him to etherealize. Soon a great force bowed my head into my lap. I did not like it, and moaned, and did wish my friend would raise my head. When I could raise it, there stood my father in front of the lounge. I was too happy to move or speak. He looked solid at first, then gradually became transparent, so that I saw the lounge behind him, and then he faded wholly away.

This dear chair is always in my home, and I think it would be nice to pass out of the fleshly tenement while sitting in it. What would I care for Napoleon's throne chair at Versailles, or for the most superb chair in the possession of American multi-millionaires, in comparison with this worn, often re-covered, old, upholstered chair?

Here I sit and wonder why in the world other people cannot be as happy as I am. I get so many sad letters from different persons. Some are mediums, who are obsessed by unworthy spirits. Some are Spiritualists—

or say they are—and yet they are afraid to die. That does seem very strange indeed. Some want to develop inspirational speaking, but they cannot, because their husband or their wife persists in going on living on the earth plane. Some are dreadfully sad because they have no soul-mate. And some say that if Kate Field can come to Lilian Whiting, why can't their friends come to them?

I fully intended to write to-day on some of the things I wrote to these sad persons, thinking to perhaps aid some readers who have similar troubles, but the pencil ran away with me, and the letter has turned out a different one from what I anticipated. Like poor Pilate, in regard to the prisoner who was too great for him—" What I have written, I have written."

Yours for humanity and spirituality.

LETTER FIFTEEN.

Reasons for Being Happy.

April 17, 1898.

To the Editor of THE BANNER OF LIGHT :

In my last, allusion was made to some of the sad persons that write to me, and the causes of their sadness. I also said that I was happy, and wondered why every one could not be the same. Even when in fear of becoming totally blind, though I of course felt anxiety on that point, I was, as now, always conscious of a deep, underlying confidence and calm that nothing can disturb or remove. So, thinking of other persons and their needs, I will try to tell the ground on which I rest.

While under the bane of the old theology I was never at rest. The doctrine that God

> " Sent one to heaven, and ten to hell,
> All for his own glory.
> And not for any good or ill
> They did before thee,"

was ample proof that there was a *screw loose* in the underpinning of the universe. The only hope from this deviltry (pardon the word, but it is appropriate,) was in accepting a Saviour from the wrath to come, of whom an enormous majority of the human race had never heard. As Dr. Shedd used to say (quoted by my brother Elnathan after he came to live with me), "We are predestinated to be saved, in order that we may be more effectually saved; and we are predestinated to be damned, in order that we may be more effectually damned." To be saved with a very small minority was unspeakably selfish, and to be in the hands of an omnipotent Deity who could treat his own creation thus was appalling.

No wonder we used to sing,

> "On Christ, the solid rock, I stand,
> All other ground is sinking sand."

The second line was true enough, in such a theology. For, if the "other ground" was such a God, we might well call it "sinking sand," and worse.

After such a pandemonium of horrors, to be brought into the clear light of the new day is enough in itself alone to make one happy every day of a life, were it as long as the storied life of Methuselah.

Of my sixty-two years of conscious identity, I have known for some ten of them that, instead of sinking sand and slippery ice placed under our trembling feet by an omnipotent and omniscient fiend, we have a solid ground on which we can confidingly and rejoicingly rest, and this ground is the constitution of the universe itself.

Love, ever working slowly, slowly, from low to a little higher, is the law of this universe, and results in the improved condition of those who desire to advance from spiritual sphere to spiritual sphere. We may have things to make us unhappy here. If so, there is a cause for this condition. This cause may be our own acts, the acts of other persons, or the acts of our ancestors. A physical and spiritual law that forever prevails is that causes produce effects. If discomfort results, instead of mourning that it is so, let us rather rejoice that law prevails. For, if the legitimate effect did not follow the cause, there would indeed, be a fatal screw loose, and we should be living in a lawless universe.

There is a book called "The Reign of Law." The source, the origin of this law, no finite being may claim to know. We may say it is a personal deity with some, an infinite personality with others, and with a great English thinker, a power that works for righteousness. We may theorize as we please, as to the source thereof. The main thing for us to do, to-day, to-morrow, and forever, is to note the bearings of universal law in the way things go on, and to learn what causes produce certain effects in our own immediate sphere of action and observation; and, as fast as we learn these lessons, to adapt our own thoughts, wishes, wills, and acts to these manifestations of law.

Resting on this, we are happy, and cannot help being happy. We may even be as happy as was Ralph Waldo Emerson. Some one said to him: "Mr. Emerson, they say the world is coming to an end." "Very well," he said, "I can do without it." Though the planet itself come to an end, the soul, a living and enduring entity, will go on in spiritual spheres; and it will rise to higher states as it notes the laws that govern progress in each successive state, and regulates itself in accordance with these laws.

Yours for humanity and for spirituality.

LETTER SIXTEEN.

Kate Field and Lilian Whiting.

April 24, 1898.

To the Editor of THE BANNER OF LIGHT:

My heart goes out in sympathy to many who write to me in the hope that I or my spirit helpers can aid them. Some live in remote places, where they can reach no medium, and they say, "If your spirit friends can come to you, why cannot mine come to me?" or, "Why cannot my loved ones reach me as Kate Field can reach Lillian Whiting?" The question is a pertinent one; and if, though Spiritualists, our own on the other side of life do not come *en rapport* with us, it becomes us to ask the reason, not in a complaining spirit, but rather to seek to remove the cause after it has been ascertained.

With regard to Miss Whiting and Miss Field, one can find sufficient cause in the nature and the course of life of each why their souls can still touch each other consciously, though one be decarnate and the other still incarnate.

Miss Field had an intrepid nature, one that could penetrate new scenes and new lines of thought, find herself at home in them, and capable of being an actor therein. For instance, when the telephone was to be introduced into England, and exhibited before the Queen, in January, 1878, she was a leading spirit in the whole affair; and not only did much toward the effect of the demonstration, but sent telegrams to many newspapers on both sides of the Atlantic, and wrote notices for the *Times*, the *Telegraph*, and the *Daily News*, so that the next day all London was informed of the particulars. This is only one event in her daily public life.

When such a woman as this found herself freed from the fleshly body, and her spiritual form in vibration with the ethereal forces of the other side of life, the same intrepidity, intelligence and push which character- ized her here, enabled her to put herself in touch with ways and means, and to impress with her personality her dear and life-long friend who is still bound to ter- restrial conditions.

As to Miss Whiting, she forms a fitting counterpart in this wonderful duet. More spiritual, with a soul more finely attuned to the invisible, with less dash, and more conservative than her friend, she is just the one for Kate Field to reach. Besides, the two loved each other dearly; both longed to know the secrets of disembodied life, and each had promised to manifest to the other, whichever passed the change the first.

I saw these two gifted women at the World's Psychi- cal Congress in Chicago, in 1893. Miss Lilian Whiting had prepared an essay entitled "And That Which is to Come." It was published in full by the *Religio-Philo- sophical Journal*, and is an interesting example of spir- itual growth As in all her later writings, as well as in the one soon to appear, she seeks to combine Biblical teachings and faith in the divine mission of Christ with the fact of spirit intercourse, and presents a noble pic- ture of the coming spiritual development of the human race.

But Miss Whiting did not read the essay herself. She deputed her friend, Kate Field, to read it for her. So we had these pure, spiritual gems presented to the Con- gress through the clear, incisive tones and the bright, graceful personality of a woman who was at home on any rostrum in the world.

Beside the personal character of these two women, there is yet another reason why "Kate Field can come to Lilian Whiting." Whatever the latter lady knows, or learns, she gives to the world in clear, attractive newspaper articles and books. The Congress of Angels, who know what they are about better than short-sighted mortals, can use her as an instrument to convey truth to the world, and she is their honored instrument.

Their delegates aided her brilliant friend to come to her in Europe, and subsequently through Mrs. Piper, not so much to gratify her, and confirm her intuition of immortality, but to reach the reading world through her.

So, dear, lonely and seeking friends, let us give out freely to all we meet the sweet water that refreshes our own soul, and ever remember that the more freely we give it out to others, the more surely will it become to us "a well of water, springing up into everlasting life."

Perhaps you cannot write a newspaper letter; but you can tell your neighbor how happy Spiritualism makes you. Perhaps you cannot now write a book; but you can be so gentle, helpful and cheerful to those with whom you dwell, that they will quietly, if not aloud, bless the Spiritualism which has wrought so sweet a fruit through you, its professor and its possessor. The freedom with which we give will increase our own receptivity, while what we hoard within our own souls shrinks away, and loses its power to bless. The higher angels, especially, aid those through whom they can reach others.

Yours for humanity and for spirituality.

LETTER SEVENTEEN.
Our State After Death Conditioned By Our Life Here.

May 1, 1898.

To the Editor of THE BANNER OF LIGHT:

A recent letter from me gave the solid ground of mental and spiritual security as being the constitution of the universe itself, and the knowledge through observation that all proceeds by law, the moving power being an all-pervading beneficence that will produce in the long run the progression of each individualized soul.

While we can rest unwaveringly on these grounds, it is not in human nature not to enquire as to the actual

home where we shall dwell after being disembodied.
Now we realize that we are on terra firma, and we do
not fear as to our physical foundation. But, may we
hope for the same reality, the same support, in short
the same actual consciousness of locality, after passing
out of the fleshly body?

Most assuredly we can; and I freely confess that if
this were not clearly settled in my own mind by my
immortal helpers, I could not be so fully sustained as I
now am. It is in order to communicate this knowledge,
so satisfying because so accordant with nature, that the
present letter is written.

At the present date, nearly a billion and a half of persons are dwelling on the surface of the planet, and a
large number of them pass out of the body every moment of time. The question is, Where do they go to?
It is not enough to say that they are souls, and can
therefore go anywhere. In fact, that statement is not
true, for it at once puts the disembodied beyond the
laws of nature.

On leaving the fleshly body behind us, or rather below us, our soul will still express itself through a natural
body, which is as real as the one of flesh. All that is
not soul is matter of some sort; and what is called the
spiritual body is as truly matter, or material, as the one
of flesh; though it is matter that cannot be perceived by
the physical senses, and is ethereal enough to respond
to the vastly quicker vibrations that belong to a more
spiritual existence.

Those who have become spiritualized enough while
here to use the spirit-body will rise beyond the atmosphere and find their congenial home beyond it. But
such can, when they wish to reach their dear ones on
the planet directly, clothe their ethereal form with matter dense enough to walk the earth "and works of love
fulfil." This is the way my father works on the earth.
But my mother, being different, comes much less to the
earth-plane, and does her work here more by influence
than by actual presence.

But the majority of those who leave the fleshly body at every moment of time are unable to use their spiritual body, which does not cohere definitely, nor respond to their efforts of will to use it, until a later period, So, as they must do something, they build up a form material enough to use, and linger on the planet until they have learned to do better.

Some of these haunt the houses where they dwelt before, some hunt up sensitives whose bodies they can use, and for this purpose frequent hospitals for the insane, large crowds of people, promiscuous circles, and even animals, through whose bodies they can express corporeally what they feel. Of course, it is the persons whose affections are with earthly scenes and passions, who are also sensitive to extraneous influences whom they seek the most ardently, and to whom they adhere with the most tenacity. But persons who are self-centered, and who seek to become more spiritual, for spirituality's own sake, need not fear them. They can even welcome their approach, because angels can reach these earth-bound souls through the words and kindly thoughts of such persons.

So, dear reader, you and I have quite enough to do: first, to self-center and spiritualize ourselves; and, second, to aid all about us to do the same. In this way will the throng that crowd yearly out of the body in an unspiritualized condition be diminished. And there is no reason for discouragement, for we are responsible only for what we can do ourselves. Besides, we can go on in this magnificent work after we pass out of the body, just as my father is now doing, and as I expect to do under his direction after passing the change miscalled death.

But I have scarcely begun to answer the query proposed at the beginning of this letter, and shall have to go on in a subsequent one to show the location of the spirit world, and the security afforded by its being in exact accord with modern astronomical science. "Whatever is true is rational."

Yours for humanity and for spirituality.

LETTER EIGHTEEN.

Our Spirit-world According to Astronomy.

May 8, 1898.

To the Editor of THE BANNER OF LIGHT:

As my last left incomplete the question as to the locality of the spirit-world, I will resume the same subject.

After becoming a Spiritualist, I noticed that many spoke of the spirit-world as being a counterpart of this. Did they mean, as their language implied, that it is another world than this, by the side of it, and certainly not it? This statement did not satisfy, and it was some time before my immortal teachers enabled me to see the actual state of the case.

The spirit-world is not another world from this; it is an expansion of this. It is around the planet, and extends very far, and yet not far enough to impinge on those of Venus and Mars, in accordance with astronomical principles that we will proceed to explain.

When a new system, the solar system for instance, is to be formed, a great whirl is brought into action in some large, unoccupied space in the cosmic ether. This action makes the inner portion of the whirl denser than the outer portion. Later, a subordinate whirl is set in motion, and its denser portion forms the beginning of the outermost planet of the system. The others come into separate form in order, some of them having subordinate lesser whirls, which produce their moons, and the sun itself always becoming smaller, with the individualization of each new planet. Our sun will be smaller yet when the next planet is made, but its orbit will, of course, not extend beyond the present sun, nor will it strike the earth according to the astronomical scare that some of the newspapers inflicted upon us last winter.

As to the comets, they came from a force generated by some erratic agent; and some struck so wildly that certain comets darted off into space and can never get home again, while others have their orbits, and return with great regularity.

Newton's laws of gravitation, as, "that its force decreases as the square of the distance increases," are mathematically correct. But instead of its being gravity that *draws*, it is the force of the whirl that *drives*. We shall continue to use his figures, and revere his genius, but the time will come when the theory of gravitation will be superseded by the fact of the vortex force.

From what precedes, we see that the spirit-world of our planet, though immense to our conception, is yet limited by the whirl that individualized the the earth. While it extends beyond the lesser whirl that formed our moon, yet it never touches those of Venus or Mars. It is not a counterpart of our earth, it is around our earth; and, as a whole, it goes ever around the sun, driven by the force of the whirl which formed it, not out of *nothing*, but out of the fine matter that pervades the universe.

Its denser, central portions make the rocks and oceans, hills and dales, and the physical portions of all animal and vegetable expressions of life. It becomes less dense, more ethereal, as one goes from the planet itself, and not an inch further can we go from the planet than we are spiritually prepared to go.

We are in the spirit-world now, but in its lowest sphere. Here we commence our individual career, and unless we become spiritual while in the body, we shall have to stay here after we get out of the body, and toil and work, struggle and strive, in order to become fit to ascend to more ethereal regions.

Nine years ago in Minneapolis the occupants of a carriage, utter strangers to me, drove to the sidewalk, where they saw me walking, and said: " Miss Judson, there seem to be two kinds of Spiritualists. Will you tell us what is the difference between them?" I had never before given the subject a thought, but instantly a power seized me, and I said: "Yes, there *are* two kinds of Spiritualists. One kind wants to drag the angel-world down to earthly conditions; the other kind wants to raise mankind up to spiritual conditions, and the latter is the kind I want to be." "Thank you," said the persons in the carriage, and drove on.

I have declared these truths, explained them, dwelt on them, in my lectures and in my writings. I have declared them fearlessly, though I knew them to be unwelcome to some.

But the higher spirits have worked through many channels, a brighter day is dawning, and the new century will see Spiritualism doing all portions of its appointed work. This work is first to turn Material-ists into Spiritualists by the phenomena; and second, to lead every Spiritualist who is worthy of the name to make individual, private soul-communion with his own the balm and strength of his hours of seclusion, and the unfoldment of the innate powers of his own soul the aim of all his efforts.

Yours for humanity and for spirituality.

LETTER NINETEEN.

Combining Church Doctrines with Spiritualism.

May 15, 1898.

To the Editor of THE BANNER OF LIGHT :

The knowledge and practice of intelligent communi-cation between the living and the so-called dead are increasing so rapidly, that we see the above marked feature of Modern Spiritualism combining with all phases of radical and even conservative belief. Spirit-ualists have long expected the church, when convinced of spirit-return, to step out of the Christian fold and

disavow the old doctrines. We have done so, many
have done likewise, and were the acts of all persons
based on similar reasoning, all would do so. But some
are so conservative, or politic, or conscious of which
side of the bread carries the desired butter, that we are
seeing all shades of even Calvinistic belief adroitly combined with spirit communion.

My thoughts have been running on this subject since
reading a pamphlet lately sent to me by some kind
friend. It is entitled "The Divinity and Personality
of Jesus the Christ, from the Fulcrum of the Spiritual
Philosophy." It is by John H. Keyser, who claims to
be a Spiritualist, and to buttress his views of " Jesus
the Christ " by communications received from
decarnate spirits coming through mediums. Among
these mediums is Mrs. Cora L. V. Richmond, and the
communicating spirits are said to be Melancthon, John
Wesley, Judge Edmonds and William E. Channing.

In accordance with these communications, Mr. Keyser
claims that Jesus Christ is the connecting link that
leads man to God, that he is the Lord and Master of
souls advanced enough to recognize him, that he is the
Saviour of the world, that when God created this planet
he gave it into the hands of his beloved Son, that Jesus
Christ is the God of this planet, and that because he
lives, we shall live also. We are even asked by Mr.
Keyser to accept the old teaching of Immaculate Conception. According to his spirits, Joseph and Mary
were the parents of Jesus, and he was begotten through
them while they were both in a deep, death-like trance,
by the Spirit of God, thus making him both Son of
God and Son of Man.

That spirits do not in general give similar reports
regarding the Nazarene is accounted for by their not
being far enough advanced to approach the sphere
where he dwells.

We think it right to place these facts before our readers, so we may more clearly see the way in which
church communicants and the clergy will manage to

combine the great natural fact of spirit intercourse, which they are *forced* to accept in this day, with old church doctrines, and thus prolong the reign of ecclesiasticism over those who choose to be thus ruled over, and who *dare not trust to God alone*.

For my part, I am a Spiritualist *in toto*. God, as revealed in the on-goings of nature, and in the constitution of the universe itself, is enough for me. I require no book, no dogma, no special medium, no particular decarnate spirit to reveal to me "the way, the truth and the life." I am grateful to all high and pure spirits who stoop to my present low estate to give me mental illumination, comfort, and strength. But they are every one of them finite, and no finite spirit is more God's child than another; nor can a finite spirit, in billions or quadrillions of years, ever see God, who is the One and also the All of an infinite universe.

The efforts made by these conservative Spiritualists will accomplish a necessary work. They build a bridge by which timorous souls can step toward the new. But their work is transitory in its effects. It will aid some of the present generation who need such props; but succeeding generations will discard such props, such crutches, and dwell in the open light of day, where many of us now dwell, and which my devoted father and mother attained after leaving the physical body. Both of them dwell joyfully in God, and both declare that Jesus of Nazareth is not God in any sense of the word, and that he is in no way the Son of God more than any other finite being.

Some will sigh to read this. Old dogmas die hard, especially when they have been wedded to ecclesiastical power, but die they must. For one I fear not to walk untrammeled in the boundless fields of intuition, resting forever as a finite soul in my source, the infinite Soul of the universe.

Dogmas arise out of thoughts. That Jesus is the God of this planet is a thought, for it places the concept of Jesus within the concept of the God of this planet.

And a thought adopted as a religious doctrine becomes a dogma.

That God is love, or, as Mr. Dawbarn words it, "Love is so much more powerful than hate," in atoms and in worlds, is an intuition, implanted innately in a finite soul by its infinite source. Intuitions do not create dogmas. Dogmas perish; intuitions abide forever.

Yours for humanity and for spirituality

LETTER TWENTY.

Music for Our Meetings.

May 22, 1898.

To the Editor of THE BANNER OF LIGHT:

It was Beranger who said he cared not who made the laws for a people, provided he could make the songs. Mr. Moody, so endowed with practical power in spite of his erroneous theology, recognized from the beginning of his public career the potent influence of music; and we well remember how Moody and Sankey, the one with his plain talk and the other with his sweet singing, went through Christendom and prolonged the reign of "orthodoxy" for two or three decades.

Politicians know this power, and campaigns have been won by the spontaneous singing of a popular song. The influence of

> "John Brown of Harper's Ferry,
>   With his nineteen men so few,
> Who frightened Old Virginny
>   Till she trembled through and through,"

was deepened and widened by the well-known campaign song, and by the majestic lines of Julia Ward Howe.

The worship of Jesus and the belief in his atoning blood lingers in many a heart, because of the simple words and tune of "Jesus, lover of my soul," and kindred melodies. And it does seem strange indeed to

go to a spiritualistic meeting, and hear those present
swell the volume of song with such words as "There is
is a fountain filled with blood," "To-day the Saviour
calls," "Wash me whiter than snow," and similar songs
presenting a false theology.

If we asked the leaders why they give out these
hymns, they would say it is because the people know
these tunes. If twenty-five copies of the "Spiritual
Harp" or the "Star of Progress" were scattered through
the audience there would be very few to sing, for it is a
small minority who can read music, and dare to let their
voices sound out alone. And many cannot see, because
they have "left their glasses at home."

When I carried on meetings a year and a half in
Minneapolis I had twenty one spiritual hymns printed
on cardboard of the durable "tough check," every one of
which went to tunes familiar to most persons. And I
took fifty of them with me in my missionary labors in
Minnesota, Wisconsin, Illinois, Missouri and Kansas.
They were simply invaluable. But there was not room
for the tunes, and so they served but a transitory purpose, though I had no difficulty in inducing the audience to sing wherever I went.

Most of the regular spiritualistic meetings I have met
have a choir, or a soloist, and if a general hymn is given
out those who sing are so few that it is depressing, instead
of inspiring as it should be. The general complaint
is that Spiritualists cannot, or will not, sing. But Spiritualists are not different from other people; they can
and will sing, if the proper conditions be supplied.

What we need for our meetings is a singing book
with plain, durable covers, on good paper, with clear,
large type for both words and music, with the songs all
adapted to progress and to spiritualistic thought, with
most of the tunes familiar to everybody, and the books
to be procured at what everyday people consider a reasonable price. Of course every one would find some
songs that he would not have put in, for tastes differ.

I have seen one compilation that contains such tunes
as "Happy Day," "Come, thou Fount," "Last Rose of

Summer," "Hold the Fort," "Martyn," "Marseillaise,"
"I'm a Pilgrim," "Annie Laurie," "Home, Sweet
Home," "Maryland," and so on; and all adapted
with words that a Spiritualist can sing with pleasure.
"Bleeding Feet" is set to "Happy Day," and I will give
a stanza:

> "Such love have we beyond the gates
>   For all the hurt and sorrow torn;
> We come when trouble e'er awaits,
>   Where pain attends from night to morn.
>   Bleeding feet, bleeding feet,
>   That give before the strain and heat,
>   The stones and roughness that they meet,
>   Of you for whom our hearts do beat,
>   Bleeding feet, bleeding feet,
>   That give before the strain and heat."

The war cloud is causing many sorrows for our fair
land; and many will need what Spiritualism alone can
give, and such a song book would reach those who can
be reached in no other way. We hope that these suggestions will take root in many towns all over the country.

Yours for humanity and for spirituality.

LETTER TWENTY-ONE.

England and the United States.

May 29, 1898.

To the Editor of THE BANNER OF LIGHT:

There are all sorts of finite souls now in existence,
differing widely from each other, being roughly class-
ified as good, bad, and indifferent. But this mode of
classifying them does not accord with the spiritual
philosophy. According to that, all souls, in all worlds
and in all eras of time, come out from infinite soul,
partake of its inherent nature, and are therefore good
in their germ. And the reason they are called good
or bad is because they are in different stages of development. In fact, none are absolutely good except thy
infinite source, and none are absolutely bad, simple

because God is infinite. Therefore, good and bad are
only relative, and what is called good in one age may
be considered base and degrading after the lapse of
five hundred years.

Charles Kingsley said in "Hypatia" that Christianity
is democratic, while Spiritualism is aristocratic. This
seemed puzzling when first read, but some acquaintance with spiritualistic thought makes this statement
clear. Christianity as expounded by Paul, and adopted
by the church at large, makes works of less account
than faith, and places the condition of Jack the Ripper
and Judas on a par with that of Mr. Moody, provided
they have accepted the righteousness of Christ for
their own. This is religious democracy.

Spiritualism, on the other hand, makes the condition
of souls differ in and of themselves, and according to
their own acts. Each soul occupies his own round on
the great ladder of progression, and mounts to the next
higher one by his own efforts, and not because he believes in someone else. The Nazerene taught this
substantially, but was painfully misunderstood by
Paul.

All are not on a par: some are better than others.
But there is hope for all ; and the place attained by the
purest and most self-denying man who ever walked the
planet, can sometime be attained by the lowest one, if
he perseveres in laboring to rise.

Besides the individual and personal development of
each soul, there is a racial development which interests
greatly those spirits whose advanced outlook enables
them to glance over ages and the progress of nations.
Our view is small, compared with theirs. Still, by
opening the inner nature, we may receive some impressions of the great truths which their minds grasp.
With vision narrowed by age and circumstance, we
sympathised with the colonial struggle to be free from
the parent country, and exulted when that was accomplished. England became jealous of our growing
power, and naughtily harrassed us, till we had to defend our rights by war in 1812. And she was not

always kind when we struggled mightily to preserve the integrity of our Nation during the Civil War.

But these were family quarrels. Sometimes the older brothers and sisters become angry with a rapidly growing, aggressive and impudent child. But after all are grown and have homes of their own, the old love comes back. They remember that the same father begot them, that the same mother bore them, that the same roof-tree sheltered them ; and this love waxes so strong that they will defend those whom they pounded, when little, against all the world.

The English people are our blood relations, and we are theirs. We share the Anglo-Saxon stock ; our lines of thought and our religion are akin. We pounded each other in 1776 and in 1812, and when she did not thoroughly sympathize with us in 1861, it cut us to the heart.

But let other nations of other races, and of other lines of thought and of differing religions, cause England's foundation to tremble by savage onslaught, and we should stand by her ; and she would do the same by us. And Germany will do the same, if she remain true to her racial instincts.

And these grand, high spirits, who see what we cannot see, well know that England and America stand for humanity, for light, for civil and religious liberty, and that their united efforts will form the great rallying-point for human civillzation. Torture for pleasure, torture for political punishment, priestly tyrrany, fetters for the human intellect, the invasion of the home by military bondage, are all obnoxious to the Anglo-Saxon mind, and from the celestial outlook, they are to fall by and by.

But throes of agony must be endured to accomplish this, and great suffering prevail during decades ot years. Still, right will at last become dominant ; Ormuzd will subdue Ahriman; and free government and free religion will allow untrammeled spiritual development over wide areas of the continents of the earth.

We do not fight Spain in revenge for her exploding

the *Maine*. We fight to free tortured Cuba, and to free the mind enthralled by priestly tyranny, and warped by bull-fights, and by the Inquisition. And alas! it is more than Spain that we shall have to fight. Let our hearts ever pulse to the higher motive. Let us look to the spiritual hills "whence cometh our help." Then will "troops of beautiful, strong angels" attend the counsels of our leaders, strengthen the arms of our militia, and show our ocean gunners how to aim, *not* because we want to avenge the *Maine*, but because we want the world to become better, and its true spiritual development to be advanced.

Yours for humanity and for spirituality.

LETTER TWENTY-TWO.

Selfishness and Love.

June 5, 1898.

To the Editor of THE BANNER OF LIGHT:

"But the greatest of these is love." On this statement, credited to Paul of Tarsus, Mr. Drummond has written his book, entitled "The Greatest Thing in the World."

In the Persian system of mythology, though Ahriman, the evil principle, is as powerful as Oromasdes, the good, yet the latter will triumph in the long run, because he can foresee the results of his own acts, which the bad one cannot do.

So, though envy and hate seem in certain crises of human action to be as powerful as love, yet love wins in the end, because those who love have a broader in-telligence. Envy sees one side, his own; love sees both sides, and he also sees the eventual triumph of good over ill.

Hate sometimes conquers by brute force, but its conquest is not permanent. The cruelly-treated horse whose mouth is lacerated by improper gear, because his driver is a brute, is conquered for the moment; but the financial loss caused by brutality retaliates in his favor after the ill-temper of his owner has wreaked its passion.

But the wise owner, who holds the confidence of his animals by being always kind as well as firm, has docile and useful creatures. Persons sometimes say wonderingly. " I wish my dog would mind me as yours does you. When I call him, he goes the other way." Well, I should think he would. Animals, children, and grown-up persons, too,

> " Will follow at your call
> If you are *always kind*."

And kindness includes not only food and shelter; it includes kind words that express real love in the heart. But sometimes persons are unkind to us, though we treat them well. In that case they are followers of Ahriman, and are so mentally blind that they do not see the results of their actions. They will be in hot water by and by; and, if we really have the spirit of love, we shall be sorry for them, and not be glad.

Some persons believe in love; but their love is all for themselves, for their family, for their town, their State, their nation. That is not love. It is a more or less diffused selfishness. Love is a bubbling spring that comes spontaneously from the inner being, and is measured, not by the worthiness or the market value of its object, but by its own strength. This kind of love makes its possessor divine. Progressive decarnate spirits have this love. Quoting from " Inspiration's Voice;"

> " We know so well, we know so well,
> Their love holds endlessly,
> In spirit-life so free."

How sad they feel when they see us wanting in love, for they see the effect on our inner nature more clearly than we ! Ah! how easy it is for selfishness to creep in! A mother sees a neighbor's child puny and pale. She calls attention to the plump rosiness of her own darling's cheeks. A person writes a successful book, and another, who cares for the furtherance of the same

cause, feels ill-tempered because he did not write it
himself. If he is a Spiritualist, perhaps he says that
the spirits have told him that he is going to write one.
A modest speaker tries to deliver a useful lecture.
Persons say to him afterwards, "I was quite interested,
but of course there was not a thing in it that I did not
know before."

Even great religious establishments sometimes show
this narrow selfishness caused by the want of love.
Some one prepares a work designed for the same use
as one of their own productions. Though their own is
not capable of doing such good as the new one, they
decry it, and do everything possible to hinder its progress. They thus show a love for self rather than love
for human advancement, which all the works were
designed to promote.

But we Spiritualists, who walk in heaven's light,
under angelic guidance, who see what the blind world
cannot see, must know well that love and love alone
will prevail in the long run, and that those who walk
contrary to its impulses are causing a warp in their
spiritual growth that will give them pain and shame
when they enter the dazzling day of the spirit-land.
Here we can partially hide the wrong we feel, but not
so there.

Oh! for a broader outlook! Oh! for more of the
spirit that will lead us to see another working for the
cause we all hold dear, in his own way, without putting
stumbling-blocks in his path because it is not our way,
or because we fear that some person may like his work
better than our own! What! profess Spiritualism, and
yet demand that all shall hew to precisely the same
line, like a row of spools cut out by the same machine!
Live, and let live. Or rather, let others live and work,
and then we can work more effectually, and live more
angelically.

Yours for humanity and for spirituality.

LETTER TWENTY-THREE.

Visits to "Orthodox" Churches.

June 12, 1898.

To the Editor of THE BANNER OF LIGHT:

When it was decided that I should live in Arlington, some good church friends told me that I could have no social status here if I should foolishly allow myself to be known as a Spiritualist. And, as the Presbyterian church is supposed to take social precedence here, they seriously advised me to connect myself with that church.

Of course I did not give this well-meant advice one moment's consideration, and I let all persons with whom I come into social and business relations know very soon that I am a Spiritualist, and the reasons therefor.

So far from hypocritically connecting myself with any church here, I have not even been to any church in town on Sunday until to-day. I have been to an evening week-night prayer-meeting five times: once to the Baptist, three times to the Methodist, and once to the Presbyterian. I have a cogent reason for preferring prayer-meetings to Sunday services. It is that being an "ordained minister of the gospel, science and philosophy of Spiritualism," it does not seem natural to me to listen only; and though my mouth must be closed at those church-meetings on Sunday, I can sometimes get a chance to speak at a prayer-meeting. I spoke with great pleasure at the Methodist meeting, and thought myself quite unorthodox, for I claimed that it was impossible for any soul to be permanently lost, as all are God's offspring; and that after getting out of this fleshly body, we shall continue, as well as here, to have our own option whether to make our bed in hell, or ascend into heaven.

On telling the good minister that I hoped I had not offended his prejudices too severely, he said he liked it well, and urged me to come often, and always speak,

And one good sister there, who has since become my friend, said my words on that occasion went with her for many days, and she had quoted them to her friends.

All the churches here are upon the hill, and among the aristocracy of Arlington, while my little home is surrounded by Swedes and Germans, in the very lowest part of the town, where the malaria walketh, and the Jersey mosquito flyeth by night, and the wicked fly putteth in his best work when the sun is above the horizon.

Some weeks ago a lady from the Presbyterian church called, and asked me if I would address the Ladies' Foreign and Home Missionary Society of that church at one of its meetings. I willingly consented, and my theme was of course Burmah, and the work of my parents there.

Before speaking, they asked me to lead them in prayer. I did so, standing, for it is several years since I could see the propriety of *kneeling* to any being, created or increate. Toward the close of my address I told them that my views had greatly changed from those of my parents while in earth life; and that I had very good reasons for knowing that their views on many points have altered since entering spirit-life. I cited the doctrine of eternal punishment, and told them flatly that in my opinion it was a wicked doctrine. But the ladies were kind to me, and voted me an honorary member of their society.

Last Friday evening I climbed the hill to attend the Presbyterian prayer-meeting, with the words of Puck on my lips:

> "I'll be an auditor,
> An actor too, perhaps, if I see cause."

I was conducted by the pastor, a man of breeding, learning, brilliant parts, and an earnest worker. The subject was the next Sunday's lesson, the seven things said by Christ on the cross.

He said Christ was not an imposter, in contrast with Voltaire and Paine, who were, the latter being a drunkard as well. He did not say that Paine was no more an

infidel than Frothingham and Minot J. Savage to-day,
and that his religious views were held by Washington,
Jefferson, and Franklin of his own day. He did not
say that Voltaire was the exponent of the whole of the
eighteenth century, which was characterized by the
spirit of free inquiry; and that this free inquiry attacked
not only religion, but politics, philosophy, moral and
physical science, government, in fact, everything; and
that the eighteenth century formed a fitting and a necessary prelude to our own.

He said that the expression " That it might be fulfilled " was a "gloss" introduced by those "saintly men "
who copied the scriptures, and excused it saying we
might have done the same in their place. When he said
words in the Bible were a gloss, I recognized the effect
of the higher criticism, and was reminded of Dr. Briggs
at Union Seminary.

The meeting was finely and effectively carried on, on
the basis of the supernatural character of Jesus, and the
atoning efficacy of his blood. The climax of feeling
was reached by singing the following words, to the exquisite old melody of Annie Laurie:

> " There is constant joy abiding
>   In Christ, my lord and king ;
> Of his love that passeth knowledge
>   My heart and tongue shall sing.
> He is all in all to me,
>   And my song of praise shall be
> Hallelujah, oh my Saviour,
>   I am trusting only thee. "

The evangelical church holds to these two points,
the miraculism of Jesus, and the blood atonement,
just as strongly as ever, in spite of the admitted
"errancy" of certain passages in the Bible. For that
reason I cannot be a member of any evangelical church.
And I cannot join the Unitarians because a large portion of them are materialists, and deny the natural and
scientific fact of spirit-return. With regard to continued existence without a fleshly body, their verdict is
" Not proven."

So you and I, dear, honest, and logical Spiritualist, must live and pass out without the pale of the Christian church. But we need not fear. With Spinoza, we can rest on God alone.

Yours for humanity and for spirituality.

LETTER TWENTY-FOUR.

Calvanistic Terror of Death and Hell.

June 19, 1898.

To the Editor of THE BANNER OF LIGHT:

Many advocates of Spiritualism seem to think that so many in the church have been affected by its doctrines, that the work is about done, and that church-members have, as a whole, renounced orthodoxy in their hearts. We do not think so; but think, on the contrary, that when driven by the search-light of truth from one stronghold, they entrench themselves more impregnably in another.

There is one old doctrine that has been more widely discarded than any other—the doctrine of endless punishment; and yet we know personally great numbers who adhere pertinaciously to even this. I actually know persons who felicitate themselves on the expectation that when I die, I shall learn to my cost, what hell-fire is, and that eternity will teach me that it will be endless. Of course, their opinion does not affect me in the slightest degree.

But alas! many are unable to free themselves from this terrible foreboding. I will cite a case: I know a Spiritualist family of long standing, who are intelligent and noble hearted, and live and walk joyfully under the light of the new dispensation. There was an elderly lady of means who had been brought up, like myself, as a Calvanistic Baptist. She was a great sufferer from a complication of diseases, that gave her extreme torture, and rendered her helpless. She was remarkably intelligent and well-read, and in character she was conscientious and truthful. No one could point to any wrong that she had ever done.

This invalid lady was taken into this spiritualistic family, and was cared for by them faithfully and lovingly for years and years. But they were never able to dislodge from her mind the notion that she was not saved, and was to burn eternally in hell. She thought of God as an implacable being who would punish her forever and ever with hell fire. When her minister, a strict believer in endless punishment, came to see her, her terrified inquiry was, "Will I burn? Will I burn?" Nothing brought her any relief, though her kind friends said everything possible to enlighten and calm her mind. During the last twenty-four hours that she continued to breathe, her cries and screams were heard by the neighbors without ceasing, and expressed her reluctance to die, and her dread of the burning, which she was sure was coming to her.

Poor, poor, Frances! That was some three years ago. We trust that her terrified, but pure spirit, has been consciously enfolded by loving angels who have won her to realize the green pastures and the still waters of the exquisite spirit-land.

While I carried on my school in Minneapolis, the pastor of the Westminster Presbyterian church was a good friend to me. On Fridays I used to give my pupils a long recess, and played for them on the piano while they marched and danced with great delight. This minister heard of this, and once talked to me a quarter of an hour on a street corner, entreating me not to allow them to dance, and citing the death-bed he had just attended of a young lady who suffered great remorse because she had danced at a party. He once preached at the Baptist church, which I then attended. His theme was eternal punishment, and he declared most determinedly that this suffering was punitive, and not reformatory.

This clergyman was no ignorant exhorter. He was a man of learning, taste, and humor. He later received a flattering call to New York City. The last time I went to see my brother, I saw on a beautiful church on 23d street his name as the pastor thereof, and he was thus recalled to my remembrance. He will never change the breadth of a hair on this side of Jordan. Peace to the good, pure man!

Many church people have loosened their hold on endless punishment, but they grip all the harder on the dogmas that Jesus was deity incarnate, and that his blood alone can save. They found these two notions on his miraculous character. But we can upset even these in time by constantly promulgating and reiterating the glorious truth that all phenomena, either now in America, or two thousand years ago in Palestine, are natural and have nothing miraculous about them. As people accept this fact, so simple, so true, so grand, the old erroneous notions of miracles, and incarnate gods, and resurrections of fleshly bodies, and blood washings will slip away from them.

Years ago, I used to talk about the proofs obtainable by phenomena. Now my guides teach me another way. Talking of phenomena only whets the appetite of enquirers to see what they may never see, and that circumstances might prevent their accepting if they did see it. But when we talk a great truth, as that all that is at all, is sure to be natural, and not miraculous, or that the expression "God is love" means that every existing soul will have opportunities of advancing sometime, if not now, we are appealing to their reason and their common-sense, thus giving them substantial food for growth.

Yours for humanity and for spirituality.

LETTER TWENTY-FIVE.
Personal Experiences.

June 26, 1898.

To the Editor of THE BANNER OF LIGHT:

A late number of *The Outlook* gives Susan W. Self-ridge's charming visit to Gladstone in his hiding place in Penmaen-Mawr, in which he spoke facetiously of his "cataract spectacles." I had my first pair last January for "distance," and a tiny steel pair without bows, to hook on to them, for "reading." But by April both eyes had altered so much that using them gave me pain, and besides, the vision became dimmer. I needed new lenses.

The surgeon tested my eyes thoroughly last week, said they were firmer, and that I could now have my permanent glasses. He ordered two pair—one for distance and the other for reading. I shall be able to write and sew with more ease. I must, however, confess that my left eye, "the Worcester eye," always pains me and always will except when quietly closed. It cannot be remedied, and "what can't be cured must be endured." It is not a severe pain, but it feels as if there were a cinder in it. It is the eye that broke open and lost about a third of the vitreous humor. Being allowed to heal without interference, the scar adheres to the iris and prevents it from contracting and dilating freely. *Hinc illae lachrimae.*

Some persons think that those who write books make a great deal of money. Successful novels, and such books as "Looking Backward," Mark Twain's works, and the Samantha series, bring in large pecuniary returns. But books like mine, that present Spiritualism *in undisguised form* cannot be very profitable in a money point of view. I have published all my books myself, assuming the whole of the expense. My experience is that when such books have paid for their original cost, including plates, nearly all persons have bought who

intend to buy, and the sales run low. I have, however,
been more successful than many. Many have published
works on Spiritualism that never paid for the original
cost, and the authors have been obliged to reduce them
to one-fourth the first retail price, in order to get any
of their money back. One reason I have never been
led to this last is that I put all my works as low as possible in the first place. My object has not been to make
money. My object is to get these books before the
world, anyway, and if possible to pay expenses.

Now a word as to my general health. If I keep
very quiet at home, eat onions daily, eat no pie,
cake, preserves, fat, strawberries, asparagus nor
tomatoes. I sleep well and feel tolerably well. If
I go to a meeting of any kind, and just listen
without speaking a word, I am so weak that I
can scarcely totter home. If I am away from home
three days, I become ill. I nearly died, lecturing from
place to place on the spiritualistic rostrum. I can never
do it again. I have lectured where I had to walk three-
quarters of a mile in a driving storm to the hall, and back
again to sleep (?) on a bed, one corner of which rested
on a pile of books, and which I could not make into a
more comfortable condition lest the whole thing should
come down. I have lectured where I was put at a
hotel, in cold, stormy weather, into a room that there
was no way of heating, and no blankets on the bed.
The blankets were promised, but, failing to materialize,
I went to a store late Saturday evening and bought me
a pair which I afterwards took in my trunk. I have
lectured when I had to lie nights in the sitting-room on
a broken down lounge. I have lectured when my hands
were so stiff with the cold that I could not turn over
the leaves of a singing-book. I have lectured after
being scolded at the door by the presiding officer because the audience was not larger.

I would rather live poor and alone in my home with
my two little dogs, answer the letters of kind friends,
give advice and consolation to those who come to me
for the same, teach the children around to be gentle

and kind, cook on two little oil stoves, dig weeds in the
yard, and write every week for the dear good BANNER,
than lecture itinerantly on the spiritualistic rostrum
with an admission fee of ten cents. Young women can
do it, but I am too old, too weak, and too good-for-
nothing to cater to the tastes of a spiritualistic audience. But I am happy; nothing can rob me of that.

Yours for humanity and for spirituality.

LETTER TWENTY-SIX.

Spiritual Development Better Than Mediumship.

July 3, 1898.

To the Editor of THE BANNER OF LIGHT:

The general principle that all that is at all is natural
is applicable not only to the phenomena of the Jewish
Bible, but to all the phenomena of our own intercourse
with those who have passed to a higher sphere of a
natural universe. Though very unwilling that the
clergy *per se* shall do the thinking for us, many Spiritualists are willing that mediums and decarnate spirits
shall think for them, and even use for them the divine
attribute of free will.

A medium uses powers that are wholly natural and
that are possessed in latent form by all. We therefore
claim that the first step to mediumship is to live according to natural law.

Mediumship does not necessarily mean that the person possessing it is himself in conscious relation with
decarnate spirits, or that he can commune with those
dearest to him in spirit. It means that spirits out of
the body can communicate with other mortals through
his organism.

We have known many mediums whose work gives
large satisfaction to others, who are unable to get the
slightest proof of spirit-intercourse for themselves.
One in particular, now in spirit-life, told me that he

would give any sum of money if he could know that his mother was really alive. Another medium, one of the finest for materialization that I ever saw, told me that he had not the slightest evidence for himself that our dead friends go on living, that he feared those beings who controlled him, and that he should drop the whole business if it was not for the money in it.

It is truly delightful not to be in the lecture field any more, because I can now say freely what I really think, without having hatred displayed against me. The hatred of others gives great pain to a sensitive. When in one's own little home, surrounded and enfolded by one's own guides, venomed shafts cannot penetrate the barrier they erect. But when traveling from place to place, lecturing to promiscuous audiences, the slightest hint from my lips in certain directions was enough to make some throw such an influence of opposition that I really suffered on the platform. The main things that awakened the greatest opposition were the statements that the development of one's own soul is more important than mediumship, and that is better not to be a medium than to have a low " control." Though the whole scope of " The Bridge Between Two Worlds " points to the same, it did not arouse such opposition as the spoken word, simply because these persons did not read such books.

That many successful mediums are controlled by earth-bound spirits is a fact that in time becomes clear to a thoughtful investigator. This fact is denied by some, and is declared by others not to be of the slightest consequence.

But its consequence is paramount, and it were far better never to be a medium than to be used by low, decarnate spirits, who are able to use a mortal because the soul of that mortal is in a low and undeveloped state. This is especially applicable to those who earnestly seek to develop as mediums, and make this their goal, rather than the purification and elevation of their own inner moral nature.

Why are such persons eagerly desirous of obtaining mediumship? There is one reason, and we all know it. If they did not fancy it an easy and a lucrative way of making money, their quest would be less ardent.

To show that I am, however, well aware that many seek for mediumship from high and pure motives, I will cite two instances that have come to my knowledge within two or three months.

One is of a gentleman and lady in New York City who are earnestly cultivating her gift, with the sole object of their own spiritual development, and of convincing certain dear relatives that the claims of Spiritualism are indeed true. High angels are furthering their efforts. Certain mischievous spirits who annoyed them at first are controlled and instructed, and her gift is being manifested more strongly and effectually.

Another instance is of a dear little coterie in far-away Nebraska. A boy among them was controlled by a pure and lovable spirit. One of the circle wrote me, "It was so easy to do right, to be kind and charitable and patient, when we could hear her every Saturday night." She also wrote that the spirit's words through the boy reformed several that had started down hill, and that one could not hear an oath in a week's time, while they all swore before that.

But the boy moved away, and they were very lonely and hungry. They hold together, seek for the highest, try to yield to impressions, and some are beginning to develop powers for usefulness. They would smile at the notion of making money by mediumship. They want it in order to do good and to get good. They make their living by farming, fruit-raising, and hard labor. And when Saturday night comes, they fill their cups from the fountain of everlasting life.

Pure mediumship comes under rare and specially favoring conditions. Spiritualism has been degraded by offering mediumship in promiscuous circles and audiences at ten cents or ten dollars a head.

A medium's powers deteriorate in a promiscuous circle, where the amount he makes depends on the number of persons present. This drags mediumship in the dirt and the mire, and is in our opinion the main reason why Spiritualism is not revered by the world at large. Many persons, filled with a high hope, begin to attend the meetings, but turn away disgusted.

Many raise the cry, "But mediums must live." Yes: mediums, like other persons, must have money for the necessaries of life. But let them make money in some other way, and reserve their high gift for only spiritual and congenial occasions. "But mediumship exhausts those who exercise it," say others. It exhausts them when used promiscuously, and when it is forced in order to make money. When used aright it does *not* exhaust; it replenishes the life-forces, as some of us know by our own blessed experience.

Thank you, kind Mr. Editor, for allowing me to speak through your pure columns without wearing a muzzle.

Yours for humanity and for spirituality.

LETTER TWENTY-SEVEN.

Creeds, and the Muzzling of Ministers.

July 10, 1898.

To the Editor of THE BANNER OF LIGHT :

Immersed here in America, as well as all over the world, in the struggle to make a living for self and family, in commercial, scientific, or literary pursuits, or in the quest for pleasure in varied forms, it is very easy for persons, in general, to relegate all soul concerns to those who they fancy are more capable than themselves in that direction. Those in the church leave their spiritual interests with the minister, the trustees, and the older members; worldly and political men leave them to their mothers, sisters, and wives, and many Spiritualists, overlooking the significance of the name they bear, and the cardinal claim of individuality, leave them to inspirational speakers, and to other mediums of communication between this life and the next.

To be accessible to disembodied influence, consciously or not, is perfectly natural, and, indeed, universal. Many an excess of anger or passion, and many beautiful feelings and thoughts, come to men and women everywhere from decarnate souls who are attracted to them by congenial tastes. Persons sometimes say, "I do not wish to be a Spiritualist, because I do not wish those who have died to be about me." They are ignorant that being a Spiritualist does not cause the approach of the disembodied. It only makes one more conscious of this natural fact.

Spiritualism is a fact and does not depend in the slightest on whether it is accepted or not. Many church persons, however, think their accepting it or not alters the case in hand. They are accustomed to dealing with matters in this way; for if they are Calvinists, all the world will be damned if not in Christ; and if they are Universalists, everybody will be sure to be saved at last. Instead of formulating a creed on the actual and evident facts of existence, they make their creed first, and then expect the constitution and course of the universe to square itself by that creed. O fools and blind!

All this unreason is because their ancestors have from remote ages adopted the writings of some mediumistic Jews, accessible to spirit-influences of varying degrees of intelligence and goodness, as the absolute and personal words of an omnipotent, ominiscent, and omnipresent God. This fundamental assumption is the cause of all these false and unnatural doctrines. But to this shifting rock they cling, and pathetically say: "If you take *my Bible* from me, you leave me nothing." It seems useless to tell them that God is found in nature, and that surely Infinite God must be enough for a finite soul, without the intervention of any book or any mediator. Such statements seem to frighten them.

The *Philosophical Journal* published a cute poem several months ago. It represents an old negro whose mind is greatly disturbed because his new minister does

not accept all 'the Bible stories as facts, and explains
them away by the application of modern science. Each
stanza ends with the refrain, partly pleading, partly
objurgatory, and wholly funny to an outsider, "O my
lamb!" The poem closes with the following stanza:

> "Take my Adam, take my Eve,
> Take my serpent that deceive,
> Take my Jonah, take my whale,
> And bust my religion! Poor niggah wail
>   O my lamb!"

A week or two ago a Presbyterian synod of examin-
ers of applicants for the ministry took exceptions to the
advanced views of Mr. Bebb, and refused to ordain him.
His clear intellect and absolute sincerity made them
most desirous of accepting him, but they dared not,
and he was voted down. One of the most active against
him was my old friend, the Presbyterian minister,
alluded to in my twenty-fourth letter.

And "*The Outlook*" of July 9 tells how the Congre-
gational Council at North Cambridge, Mass., advised
the church there not ordain and install William J. Long
as its pastor. They object to Mr. Long because he in-
sists that some parts of the Bible are purely legendary
or mythical; and that the salvation of all men is a
logical necessity from belief in the immortality of the
soul and the love of God. The second point is the very
one I made with a delightful coterie of Presbyterian
women here a few days ago.

It remains to be seen whether this church will settle
Mr. Long against the opinion of the Council. If not
they better go over to the Presbyterians at once, and
be ruled like them by a Synod. If they accept Mr.
Long for a year, the end of the year will find seven-
eighths of them believing just as he does. It is to be
hoped that this pure-minded, great-souled young man,
who has spent fourteen years of his life in preparation
for the ministry, will find a pastorate somewhere where
he can preach the truth, the whole truth, and nothing
but the truth. The idea of standing up in a pulpit and
talking to an audience with a muzzle on! It is bad

enough for dogs to wear them, but for a human being
to wear one is, as Dogberry says, "Most intolerable
and not to be endured."

Turning to another subject, and led thereto by the
power of association, I will tell you of something
else. Arlington is a part of Kearney, where Clark's
thread is made. Early in June, at the noon hour, when
the teacher was away, a small, hungry dog entered the
schoolhouse, hoping for something to eat. The boys
set on him, beat him, kicked him from corner to corner,
and threw him among the little girls. At last he became frenzied with fright and pain, and bit two little
girls. Then a policeman came and shot him. Then
Arlington and Kearney had a mad-dog scare, held a
town-meeting, and voted that from July 15 to October
15 every dog on the street without a wire muzzle around
his nose can be killed by anybody. So the law allows
a crowd of cruel boys to mob and kill such a dog, thus
fostering the murderous instincts implanted in the
human breast by a remote ancestry, but supposed to be
gradually eradicated by civilization.

A muzzle is a cruel appliance. It prevents the mouth
from perspiring freely, the mouth being the natural
canine place for the perspiration to flow. Humane
owners will keep their pets in the backyard and the
house until these calamities be overpast, and subject
them to the muzzles only when really necessary.

I never met such stringent laws before, but then I
never before lived in New Jersey. It is hoped that the
New Jerusalem will be different. To be sure, the Bible
says: "Without are dogs," but the *revised* heaven will
allow those who like animals to have them, while those
who dislike them will never see a dog or a cat in the
pretty homes the other side of the shining river.

Yours for humanity and for spirituality.

LETTER TWENTY-EIGHT.

Magnetic Harmony.

July 17, 1898.

To the Editor of THE BANNER OF LIGHT:

Many writers on occult subjects misapply the word
magnetize, using it where *mesmerize* is the proper term
to use. To mesmerize, psychologize, or hypnotize any-
one is for the operator to temporarily control the subject, so that he will do the acts, speak the words, and
see the sights impressed on his brain by the one who
controls him. The force exerted being a mental one,
it can be exercised by embodied or disembodied spirits
on incarnate or decarnate persons.

One who has yielded to this control when wielded
by a mortal passes more readily under the sway of a
disembodied intelligence. Such a person is a sensitive or a medium. In this way, mesmerizers have
frequently made their subjects mediumistic. It was
through such a human instrument that A. J. Davis
originally went under the control of a disembodied
intelligence, who wisely discarded after a time the
assistance of a human operator.

While a person desiring to be controlled by a spirit
can often settle his capability in this direction by seeing if a mortal can mesmerize him, yet many who have
never been mesmerized are mediumistic to the extent
that they can be sufficiently psychologized by spirits to
see visions and receive impressions from the spirit-side
of life. I belong to this second class. No mortal has
ever been able to mesmerize me completely, but my
father and other guides often assist me to see visions
in spirit-life and to drink inspiration from the infinite
fountain of intelligence.

To return, some persons say *magnetize* when *mesmerize*
is the right word, from the fact that a magnet attracts
to itself particles of iron, and the mesmerizer can draw
his human subjects to himself if he so wills.

But this attraction is not exerted in the same way. The mesmerizer, psychologizer, or hypnotizer draws his subjects to him by the exertion of his will, which is temporarily or permanently stronger than theirs. It was in this way that Leonora de Concini controlled Mary de Medici in the early part of the seventeenth century. Before being executed as a sorceress, she was asked how it was that she could so sway the queen-mother. "By the power of a strong mind over a weak one," was her haughty reply.

It is not in this way that a magnet draws iron particles to itself. It is because the magnet itself vibrates in unison with the great earth-magnet ; and when the small particles are brought near it, they begin to share in the same vibration and pass to the magnet, which is larger than they.

It may be asked what we mean by magnetism. The answer is simple. Every atom in the universe has both kinds of electricity in it. When these two kinds of electricity pass to the opposite poles of the atom, it is in the magnetic state. Electricity is a force, while magnetism is a condition.

What is true of an atom is true of aggregations of atoms, as organized beings, and the earth itself. In the great mother-magnet, the earth itself (we say mother, for she is the mother of our corporeal frames), the negative electricity goes to the north or negative pole, while the positive kind goes to the south or positive pole. We call the north pole negative because the positive end of the magnetic needle turns to the north ; and every tyro on these subjects knows that if a small, free magnet be placed against a larger one, its positive end will seek the negative end of the larger one, and *vice versa*.

The earth being in the magnetic condition, is in the healthful, harmonious, and thoroughly proper state that a planet should be in. And what is true of the planet itself, is true of that far larger world which surrounds the earth, extending far, far out into space, of which the earth is the minute nucleus. This is the spirit-world of the earth, the successive spheres of which will be the homes of all human souls during countless eons of time.

This enormous spirit-world has its poles, and is of course in a magnetized condition, and only those souls whose forms vibrate in harmony with the same are able to pass on in its successive and more exalted spheres.

These natural facts have great importance in our present daily life. It is quite impossible to have health of any kind, and healthy mediumship is one of these kinds, unless our physical body and our spiritual body are in the magnetized condition that makes them vibrate harmoniously with the earth and with the greater spirit-world. Magnetic inharmony is the cause of disease, both physical and mental, and to harmonize the bodies of the soul with external nature, as well as the soul itself with Infinite Soul, is the most important thing for each to do.

So deeply do my guides feel this that they have for ten years sought through me to carry to others what is in their opinion the best method to harmonize the fleshly and the spiritual body with universal nature and the soul with universal soul. The first years were devoted to teaching me enough to begin to teach.

In 1890 I began to teach others, by lessons, at Clinton Camp, and by directions printed in five Spiritualist papers. The lessons have been given in many cities and towns. In 1891 " Terrestrial Magnetism " was published ; and the directions therein, with a vast amount of elucidatory matter, were published in 1894 in the work named by angels, " The Bridge Between Two Worlds."

My aim has been to reach as many as possible. Much has been accomplished. Many all over America walk in this path, and we have yet to learn of any who have tried these methods faithfully and persistently who have not derived benefit therefrom. The only trouble has been with some correspondents who paid more attention to the physical processes than to the spiritual ones, thus opening the door to an undesirable class of spirits. The motto of my guides has ever been, "Purity, first; mediumship, second."

The greatest obstacles we have met are from some Spiritualists who already fancy that they "know it all," from some mediums who are antagonistic to the spirit of the motto cited above, and from a class of persons who think that all spiritualistic development should deal with the soul alone, and have nothing to do with the body itself. But, as whatever is true is sure to survive and conquer, we have no fears regarding the ultimate success of these teachings.

Yours for humanity and for spirituality.

LETTER TWENTY-NINE.

Sanitation: Kindness to Animals.

July 24, 1898.

To the Editor of The Banner of Light:

I spent the latter days of my childhood with the relatives of Ann H. Judson, in a quiet New England town near the Merrimac river. All who lived in this region in the olden time remember the sudden and seemingly sporadic cases of tuberculous consumption, and the epidemics of typhoid fever to which it was subject. Calvinistic Congregationalism was the prevailing religion; and when a person died from these or other diseases, the event was thought to be a dispensation of Divine Providence. I well remember how after a death the minister would solemnly read from the high pulpit that Mr. and Mrs. So-and-So requested the prayers of God's people that the late afflictive dispensation might be sanctified to their spiritual good. Then the whole family stood up in their pew while the special prayer was made.

All these people thought that sickness and death came as a special expression of divine sovereignty, and were not to be prevented or even accounted for by science. Afflictions were chastisements from God's own hand, and to be borne in meek submission, while we "In God's hottest flame stood still." Whatever happened, he did it, and we were in no way accountable.

The family where I lived had several cases of typhoid fever, and it never occurred to them that the well opening into the kitchen, and very near the deep cesspool, had anything to do with it. God, in his mysterious ways, for their spiritual improvement, or in chastisement for their worldliness, saw fit to send these illnesses upon them.

These diseases are less prevalent in this region than in the old days, for people have learned more of the laws of sanitation, and of the absolute necessity of keeping the water beyond all contact below or above ground with any disease germs.

Some of us remember the dreadful attacks of typhoid fever to which the Prince of Wales was subjected. The drains at Sandringham Palace were overhauled, and yet he was again very ill. Then by severe scrutiny it was found that there was a connection between the drinking water and a distant reservoir of disease germs. This was corrected, and there was no more illness at the palace

Last winter there was an epidemic of typhoid fever in the town where I live, and many died. It was found that the milk from a certain milkman came from cows who drank infected water, so they took no more milk from him. I always sterilize milk before using it. This is easily done by heating it to a point when "the wrinkled skins of scalded milk" begin to show on the surface, without allowing it to actually boil. No person, certainly no little child, should swallow milk that has not been sterilized ; unless we know not only that the cow is healthy, but that she eats pure food and drinks pure water. Had I dreamed that the people here did not use proper precautions, I should have obtained two hundred copies of "The Milk Question" and left one at every house.

While the epidemic was at its height, I strayed into the Methodist prayer-meeting, and was amazed to hear the pastor allude to one of these deaths as an afflictive dispensation of divine Providence, and ask all to pray that the loss might redound to the spiritual benefit of the relatives, and thus enhance the divine glory. I felt a good deal like saying a few words, but feared it might be an intrusion.

So far no doubt many of my readers may agree with me, but perhaps in what I have next to say, they will think I am going too far. But I would much rather go too far than not far enough. "But because thou art lukewarm, I will spue thee out of my mouth."

To proceed, I don't like the notion of drinking milk that comes out of an animal. The baby takes its mother's milk, and it does it good, provided the mother is thoroughly healthy, sweet-tempered, and wise. But it repels me to think of drinking what comes out of the udder of a cow. And besides this personal feeling of aversion, I think we have no right to take her milk.

The cow's milk comes to the creature from wise Mother Nature, in sufficient amount to nourish her offspring. And the calf receives it when hungry, which is very often. This is natural, and is therefore just as it should be. But human beings, who have a larger brain, that they use for tyranny and not for beneficence, put the cow into an unnatural condition. By breeding and special culture, they develop her milk-forming organs unnaturally. When the calf is born, instead of letting her rear it lovingly and naturally, they take it away from her; and her pitiful lowings when thus bereft give pain to a feeling heart. Giving her food and treatment to increase the amount of milk, they are yet so cruel as to relieve her of it only twice in twenty-four hours. I have been many times waked up on Sunday morning by the distressful cries of cows, who were suffering because the man came late to milk them. And they often begin to low for relief at three in the afternoon. but have to wait till they are called at six. All this is unnatural and painful as well as very selfish on the part of human beings.

If only those marry who are fit to marry, and if men
and women were so normally spiritual as to have only
their two children, the mother could nurse her own
child, and not depend on a lower animal. What kind
of a man or woman the baby makes depends greatly on
his sustenance in his early years as well as in the months
before birth. If this sustenance comes directly from a
healthful, intelligent, and spiritual woman, his moral
and his spiritual nature have a better setting than that
which comes to him by these unnatural by-paths.

It is distressing to a feeling heart to hear the cries of
an animal in either mental or physical pain. In Eureka,
Kan., on my way to the hall on Sunday, I passed an
enclosure where a mare was running around and
screaming at the top of her voice, because they had
just taken her own colt away from her. I had to go on
to meet my engagement at the hall, and her screams
died away in the distance. While lecturing one Sunday
in Baraboo, Wis., policemen were killing a dog in the
yard below. I had to cease speaking until his agonizing
death cries had died away.

Last Friday a little dog jumped from a second story
window to get away from his new master. I gathered
him tenderly in my arms, carried him home ; and, as
he was suffering greatly, I put him to sleep with strong
chloroform. He will never suffer any more.

Druggists are not allowed to sell such chloroform
without a physician's prescription. But I always get
it through some medical friend, and keep it on hand
for such emergencies as these. Shut the animal in a
tight box, and at once put in a large rag saturated with
chloroform, and cover the box well in a room with
closed windows. Do not open the box for twelve hours,
unless it seems necessary to put in more chloroform.

Yours for humanity and for spirituality.

LETTER THIRTY.

The Basis of True Philosophy Must be Simple.

July 31, 1898.

To the Editor of THE BANNER OF LIGHT :

Among the noblest words in our language are the adjective simple, and its noun, simplicity; while their converse, double and duplicity, are of another character. Simple is probably derived from *semel*, once, and *plicare*, to fold, and so a simple thing is easily understood. But when a thing is double, from *duo*, twice, and the verb, its ins and outs are so complicated that it is not easily seen through, if at all. As to duplicity, it is a noxious manifestation of character that must be discarded by one who seeks spiritual growth.

But the vain world is apt to regard what is simple with scorn, and in fact a simple person has become synonymous with simpleton.

Still, the truly great is the most truly simple, and the best teacher is he who can present a thought or a truth so clearly and simply that the pupil wonders that he never saw it before. And the best lecturer is not he who befogs the audience and leaves them "in wondering mazes lost," but he who tells the truth so simply and clearly that the wise listener drinks it in as the flower-cup drinks in the refreshing dew, though the ignoramus declares, " Not much, I knew it all before."

Philosophy, science, metaphysics, and religion have been presented in such complicated forms that common people shrank back aghast, and said that only the learned and the deep were able to understand them. In this way, the vanity of those who expounded them was flattered. Such were the teachings of many ancient philosophers and of the Pharisees. But the plain talk of Socrates was listened to by the poor cobbler as well as by Alcibiades, while it was said of Jesus that "the common people heard him gladly."

To be able to teach in this way, several things are necessary. One must see for himself, with absolute clearness, what he desires to communicate to other minds; he must be willing to use simple language and not seem learned at all, he must enter the mind of his pupils and see the difficulties as they arise in their minds, and in fact he needs true human fellowship and sympathy.

Basic facts are never complex; they are simple. Complicated effects may arise as they work into practice, but in themselves they are direct and simple. The universe itself is the expression of the most simple fact. This underlying and all-permeating fact is that all that there is, is matter and soul. The soul is, anyway, and expresses itself by matter. Infinite soul expresses itself in the infinite universe, and finite souls express themselves in plants, in animals, in human beings, and in spirits. There may be less developed finite souls that express themselves in crystals and rocks. That may be so, but as I do not see that clearly, I cannot teach it.

An atom, if such things exist, is not a finite soul; nor is an infinity of atoms the infinite soul. Atoms, hypothetically existing, are matter, and souls express themselves by them, singly or in the aggregate. An atom is not an ego, but an ego uses it or them, in order to manifest itself to other egos. This is Spiritualism, and the contrary is materialism.

Soul is eternal; it has always existed, and will always exist. If matter has always existed, it has done so merely as an expression of the soul itself. Whether matter is eternal, as well as soul, is beyond the knowledge of every finite being. We may, however, have our opinion on that point, though of course it may change in the course of eons of time. My present personal opinion is that infinite soul is back of the ultimate atom. For atom one can of course substitute any other term, according to the scientific school that he adopts at present.

My guides have never taught me to speak of infinite spirit. To call God spirit is misleading and illogical.

Spiritualists call their decarnate friends spirits, and we call mortals in the flesh men, women, and children. We call them so, because they appear to be such to the eyes of a mortal. In the same way a spirit appears to be such to the vision of a spirit. A spirit is a manifestation of the soul within, the real ego. That soul we do not see, either here or there. We see the manifestation of it. The spiritual body, or the spirit, is one thing; the soul is another.

Such misuse of terms employed arises from an original want of clearness in our conceptions. And having formed the habit, many continue, and thus bewilder those who are entering on the study of Spiritualism.

The constitution of a human being is, to our present view, very simple. Whether in the body or out of the body, we are dual, and the two constituent elements are soul and form. But, before transition, the form is itself dual. Here, or rather in, we have our fleshy body and our spiritual body, though the former is the obvious one, under ordinary conditions. And we know, by looking at the face of this body, whether the soul within is truthful or deceitful, loving or malicious, because the soul *expresses* itself by it. So a human being here is constituted of indwelling soul, spiritual body, and fleshly body.

When there, or rather out, the soul expresses itself only through its spiritual body, and so reveals itself more freely and unerringly. So a human being there is constituted of indwelling soul and spiritual body.

Let us not say spirit, when accurate thinking shows that we should say soul. And, as it is never too late to mend, let us begin to speak aright, and so avoid misleading those who need our help. Whether we be on the very lowest round of the spiritual ladder, or far advanced in spiritual experience, let us change our old practise, if it has been wrong, and use exactly the terms that express our own clear mental vision, and convey it in its heavenly purity to those who are looking to us for instruction, for counsel, and for inspiration.

When we go to a materializing séance, we do not see spirits unless we be clairvoyant. We cannot see spirits with fleshly eyes, we see materialized forms But many become temporarily clairvoyant at such séances, and this is the reason that some of the manifestations are seen by only a part of the audience, while the others do not see them at all. If there be skeptics among the latter, they naturally suppose that those who say they see such forms are either lying, or are hallucinated or imaginative. But all things come to those who wait; and what is founded on nature and fact will certainly survive, and be accepted by all mankind in the course of time.

In spite of the frauds created by commercial mediumship, yet materialization, slate-writing, trumpet voices, and all the other phases are used at times by decarnate spirits to prove to a doubting world that souls can and do survive the change called death.

Yours for humanity and for spirituality.

LETTER THIRTY-ONE.

Three Ways to Communicate with Spirits.

August 7, 1898.

To the Editor of THE BANNER OF LIGHT:

One of the strangest things connected with our Cause is the number of Spiritualists who are, after all, uncertain whether its claims are true. They are sometimes blamed for still seeking for tests, but the real reason they want them is because they are not certain that the departed can prove their existence by communicating intelligently with us. As a drowning man will catch at a straw, so they will run to hear every new test medium and have a sitting with each new instance of development, in the hope of getting a test that will stand by them.

As the proud claim is made that we have graduated out of believing into knowing, it does seem a pity that with so many this " knowledge " is so uncertain, and so easily shaken to the foundation. I can truly say that since I had definite communication with my father, in December, 1887, I have never for a moment doubted his individual existence and his ability to reach me at certain times. I do wish it were in my power to reach these uncertain Spiritualists, and aid them to a surer footing. Many appeal to me for this kind of help, and many letters go out from this little sanctum in the effort to comfort by fortifying their doubting souls.

One cause of this uncertainty is in the settled notion that we can know nothing unless our knowledge is on a physical basis. Many think that they cannot know of a spirit except through the physical senses of sight, hearing and touch. If we consisted wholly of a fleshly body and nothing else, that might in some sense be true.

One of the basic facts spoken of in our last letter is that we are constituted of soul and of a spiritual body and a fleshly body. This fact, so universally accepted by Spiritualists, is adopted and then laid aside as having no special bearing on our relations with our dear departed. But it has, in fact, everything to do with the communication between the two sides of life. A common mistake is in thinking that we can have real knowledge of spiritual existence only through the physical senses.

One will declare : " Why, I *know* that my mother exists, because I saw her, heard her voice, and felt her, at the séance the other night." Then when some one says that that form was made from the elements of the medium's body by her control, and that this control may have caught from this friend's mind the appearance and voice of his mother, he either contests this notion, or plunges into a sea of uncertainty, and fears that after all he did not *know* that it was his mother.

Another has *knowledge* that spirits exists, because writing came on the slates that were out of the reach of the medium. Such a one read my letter in THE

BANNER of April 16, where allusion was made to slate-writing being sometimes produced by incarnate as well as by decarnate beings, and wrote me that I had now taken away the last prop from under Spiritualism. This was not correct, however, as I was myself as firm a Spiritualist as ever, and also felt and still feel sure of having received *slate writing* from decarnated spirits.

The better way is to open the doors of the mind wide to all the facts, with their premises and inferences; and being grounded in the fact that individuality continues, and that communication takes place, we shall not be disturbed when we gradually find that we did not understand everything about the phenomena from the very first.

I think we claim too much when we say we know a thing because we have seen, heard, or touched it. I am free to say that the only thing I really know personally is the existence of my own mind. Reasoning from this one bit of knowledge, I *believe* that there is an infinite ocean of intelligence beyond and outside of me; and that there are any number of finite intelligences with whom I have communicated or may communicate in the future, through the medium of my physical and spiritual senses. The first belief is founded on intuition; the second, on the testimony of these two sorts of senses. When we think that we know anything beyond this, my impression is that we delude ourselves.

Let me never lose sight of certain points, by means of which the universe of thought and feeling coheres for my individual self. I am a soul, a finite one now, but with infinite possibilities, as I sprang from an infinite soul. This soul of mine expresses itself, now and temporarily, by a fleshly body, and now and for a far longer period by a spiritual body.

This soul of mine receives direct impressions from its infinite source, and also from a very few finite souls, either excarnate or decarnate, who are akin to it by spiritual affinity. And these impressions are more reliable, and therefore more valuable, than what comes to me by the indirect means of my spiritual body and my physical body.

A secondary and an indirect means of communicating with me is through the senses of my spiritual body, as clairvoyance, clairaudience, and clairsentience. These come mostly from decarnate spirits, and they are more reliable than those that come through my fleshly body.

A third and a still more indirect means is through the fleshly body. This is used mostly by incarnate spirits, and there are varieties, as talking, writing, facial expression, gestures, and so on. Excarnate spirits use these very indirect means to communicate with mortals when they cannot come through the spiritual senses on account of their undeveloped condition.

Another very indirect means is through a medium. Here we are hampered by the mentality of the medium, which hinders a correct picture by his own preconceptions. If it comes through the spiritual senses of the medium, it is better than through the movement of physical objects. But we have no wish to complain. Instead of wondering that communications through another are no better, let us rather be surprised that they are as good as they are.

As to fraud, we have only this to say : We have had unusual facilities for examining all the phases through many mediums, and we have very rarely found intentional fraud. We have, however, found much that looks like fraud, but which we believe comes from the medium's deluding himself or herself, or being deluded by his control. We have found sincere mediumship which was, however, hampered by the opinions and prejudices of the medium. And we have found bright examples, like "gems of purest rays serene." But these last were mostly where they were manifested without a view to pecuniary gain.

When spiritual gifts are exercised for earthly gain, their purity is tarnished. The reason is obvious. The gaze of the seer is fixed on two things, the spiritual vision and the money. The vision is distorted, the picture is not a true one. True mediums have told me

this. Of course those who do it for gain say differ-
ently. But they speak from self-interest, and we must
receive their opinion *cum grano salis*.

Yours for humanity and for spirituality.

LETTER THIRTY-TWO.

Loneliness Banished by Spiritualism.

August 14, 1898.

To the Editor of THE BANNER OF LIGHT:

When persons remain in the old orthodoxy, they of
course believe that they continue to live after the body
dies, on the ground of the resurrection of Jesus. They
have had no real evidence of continued existence; but
as they are not accustomed to receiving *evidence*, this
belief satisfies them, and they do not know what they
miss. Even the thought of death is sweet to many of
them; for they believe so firmly in the pervasive personality of Jesus, that they think he will be with them
in the dying hour, and receive them in his arms when
they have died. We do not especially pity this class,
for they often lead lovable lives, and are content.

But we do pity those who have discarded the omnipresent personality of Jesus, and the deific inspiration
of the Hebrew Scriptures, and yet have no faith in the
claims of Spiritualism. These poor souls have lost
what they once possessed, are sunk in the slough of
materialism, and are ready to say with the worldly-wise
Solomon, "The living know that they shall die, but
the dead know nothing at all." Many Unitarians belong to this class, and we are sorry for them, because
they keep their eyes fast shut against the beautiful
light that now shines throughout our beloved land.

For the same reasons, the writings of George Eliot
seem very sad to me. That high-aspiring but groping
soul lived to do good, and inculcated and practiced an
enthusiasm for humanity equal to that of the Nazarene,
but she was never assured that we retain our individu-

ality. She thought it more than likely that we are but momentary bubbles on the great sea of time, destined to glance in the sunlight for a little while, and then to be lost in the submerging waves. Her motto was, " Let us love one another, let us do all the good we can, for to-morrow we die."

" Robert Elsmere" is less sad than George Eliot's writings, but one can sigh for that pure and humane young clergyman who gave up so much because he bravely followed where the unerring logic of human history and testimony led him, and yet could not see clearly that there is a natural life to come.

A little book by Beatrice Harraden, "Ships that Pass in the Night," is so great a favorite with me that I read it every few weeks. But this pen-picture of the experience of suffering souls has the same note of uncertainty regarding "that which is to come." The writer pictures humanity as always building bridges between the living and the dead. She says each bridge proves unreliable, and then they go to work and build another one. It is a pity that she cannot see what reason and science teach so clearly in this last decade of the present wonderful century.

All the bridges between life and death, that I spent so many years in building, came to grief. The piers of some were sayings in the Old and New Testaments ; others were Plato's reasonings for immortality; another was the perpetual wish to live forever :

" Perhaps the longing to be so,
Helps make the soul immortal."

But none of these bridges lasted me. They were all swamped and buried in the sea of time, and I came to think we were not likely to personally survive the savage onslaught of that universal conqueror called Death.

But, most fortunately for my individual self, there came to me testimony eleven years ago that was so convincing that all doubt fled away, and I began to build a new bridge between that which is and that which is to come. The first pier of this bridge was the testimony of my great and noble father, who was the soul of truth and honor while here, and who can never be otherwise. The second pier was the undying love of my angel mother. The bridge then built has never swerved the breadth of a hair. I often walk on it; and by and by I shall walk clear to the other end, and pass from this fleeting and unreal life to the permanent and the real life beyond.

I have spoken of the two piers which I saw at first. These are beautiful, strong, and true. But there is a deeper, grander one, which I did not see at first, on which the first two really rest. This majestic, plummet-sounding and heaven-scaling pier is the constitution of the universe itself, which is the expression of infinite, beneficent life.

My heart swells when I think of the solidity and the grandeur of this basic fact. And oh, how I wish that I could communicate this absolute certainty to every doubting soul now on the planet! The door is open. Some see the door, but they think that it is shut for them. Others do not believe there is any door at all.

I am glad that George Eliot knows now from happy experience the life beyond the portals of the grave. And many Robert Elsmeres pass to the exquisite morning land every year, and expatiate in those happy fields. As to Beatrice Harraden, I know not if that be her real name or not, nor whether she be still on the earth-plane of life. Whoever she may be, I hope that she will yet be happy even here in knowing that there *is* a bridge, that it is secure, and that we shall surely walk on it into the city not made by hands.

She puts some most touching words into the mouth of her heroine. Said Bernardine to the Disagreeable Man: "If I believed in God as a personal God, I should be inclined to think that loneliness were a part of his scheme : so that the soul of man might turn to him, and to him alone."

All have felt that loneliness. Our bodies hide our souls from each other. Talk, "like the crackling of thorns under a pot," *hinders* the transmission of thought.

But we who are beginning to learn what Spiritualism really is, cannot be lonely any more. We are indeed alone, as a general thing, so far as persons in the flesh are concerned. But when in quiet solitude, the door swings open, and then freed souls come to the imprisoned one, and give us companionship, love, and inspiration.

When finite soul touches finite soul, without the intervention or the interference of either fleshly or spiritual body, comes an experience which is real indeed. "Soul to soul, like blending of light, will our souls mingle." My father wrote me that once. I could not believe it then, but it has come true.

But, sweet as is the companionship of finite souls, there is a still more intimate bond. It is that which binds each finite being to the infinite soul on whom it depends, and out of whom it sprang into individual consciousness He who has begun to realize this has begun to be truly happy. And, as individual existence is possible only on the basis of the existence of infinite life, so all the facts and phenomena of Spiritualism and of spirit-communion are possible only on the basis that all finite souls come from the same source. Could it be otherwise, it would be forever impossible for souls to understand one another. But as they grow toward the common parent will they come nearer to each other, and realize more fully the sweetness of existence.

Yours for humanity and for spirituality.

LETTER THIRTY-THREE.

Inspiration in Writing and Speaking.

August 21, 1898.

To the Editor of THE BANNER OF LIGHT :

As I review the way in which I have been led, seeking thereby to gain lessons for those I may now be able to reach, I note how quickly the angel world sought to bring me back to the realization of the fountain of infinite life. During the first year after my parents and other friends had proved to me their individual existence, I sought no more, and rested content in this sweet knowledge. But by the end of that year I was led to a mode of development that has for its first principle the dependence of each and all upon an infinite source, the kind of development that it is the object of all my efforts to communicate to others.

It is an absolute fact that those who walk in spiritualistic paths, and miss this great truth, are hampered in their progress ; and many, thinking that there is no infinite source in Spiritualism, enter other lines of soul-thought. Those in our ranks who claim that the knowledge that mortals continue to exist when denuded of the fleshly frame and can still communicate with mortals, is all there is to Spiritualism, are the very ones that hinder the progress of our Cause. I have met hundreds of them who make spirit existence and communion the be-all and the end-all of Spiritualism. It may be at present sufficient for them, but it is not sufficient for me. There must be both room and cause for endless growth, and this can come only by a reaching toward that which is infinite.

I was delighted, and ought not to have been surprised this last week on receiving a letter from one of our most able and original thinkers to learn that coming into conscious communion with the Infinite Parent is the groundwork of his process of development. He has been reading "The Bridge Between Two

Worlds," and, though the formulae he employs differ somewhat from those that were taught to me, yet the thing in itself is the same as that explained in chapter eight of the book just adverted to. Those familiar with the work remember that the subject of the very first chapter is "The Soul's Relation to Infinite Soul."

That book is a constant surprise to me, and an evidence of inspiration. I never planned the scope of the work, nor a chapter in it, nor read any previous chapter until the whole was completed. Then on reading it, I was amazed to see the orderly and coherent sequence of all. Many have praised the logical and philosophical mode of procedure. But as I did not plan it at all, the commendation is due to those wise spirits who planned it and employed me as their instrument. Still, we admit that unless they had found similar qualities in the writer, it would have been impossible for them to have used her brain. Neither could they have created the style. That came into being during many years of mental training, when a teacher and a member of the church.

It is to me a source of extreme gratification that what I am and what I have acquired are employed in this most glorious Cause. And I am thankful every day of my life that sufficient mediumship has been developed for angels to use my powers freely in order to give out what they desire to give. I am deeply grateful and inexpressibly happy to be used by such spirits.

I have wholly given up ever thinking what is to be the subject of any of these weekly letters. As when in the lecture-field I pay attention only to physical preparations and to maintaining a quiet mind. There are no interruptions for me on Sunday, and after dinner, with my study in perfect order, and my desk cleared of all debris, with penknife sharpened and pencils ready, having gone through the dear process of harmonizing my physical and my spiritual body with the magnetic currents of the solar system, and my soul with the higher souls of the spirit-world in the name

of the infinite source of all, I am ready to write. Even
my two little dogs, who are ready to bark at the slightest provocation on all other occasions, seem to drink in
the spirit of the hour, and are quieter than mice until
I get on to page fourteen of the manuscript, and am
ready to stop. Then they have a jubilee, and we three
children are ready to play. At supper I have my one
weekly indulgence, a cup of nice coffee.

I am as fond of coffee as is a parrot, if it has plenty
of milk and sugar in it; but it has a tendency to make
me what a certain medium accused me of being chron-
ically—" biljus." By the way, why cannot the controls
of some public mediums use ordinary English? It is
as great a mystery, inexplicable in its inscrutability, as
some of the tenets of Calvanistic orthodoxy. And
why are some controls so discourteous? We do not
like to be brow-beaten, sat down upon, and stamped
upon by mortals, and I do not see why we should bear
it from one because he is decarnated. It is my individual opinion, and of course I count as only one, but
I fancy that such mediums are more careful to humor
their controls than to put themselves into conscious *rapport* with the Infinite. That may explain the character
of much which comes through them.

I am quite tired of hearing that Thomas Paine was
an atheist. Because some one is called an infidel, he
is accused of atheism. Paine was a devout man, with
real reverence for God. And why did some one write
a work entitled " Thomas Paine: Was He Junius?"
If I were asked the question, I should reply, " Decidedly
not." Junius was vituperative, sarcastic, envious, and
malevolent. I made a study of his works at one time,
and I find his spirit quite the opposite of Paine's. Yet
it is common to say that a speaker who gives a vituperative lecture is controlled by Paine. I think he must
either smile or feel sad at such assumtions.

It seems to me a mistake for inspirational speakers
to claim certain well-known writers or statesmen as
their controls. Those really familiar with the writings
or lines of thought of these celebrities fail to discover

evidence of their real personality, and prejudice is created.

It often comes from a wish to startle, to dazzle, and in some cases to impose on the audience. It makes no difference who says a thing. What is said is the main point. Besides, the names that men account great in their day often have less real merit than the humble, unknown ones who lived at the same time ; while those who are called great, and are really great, have so marked a personality that it is a risky business to claim to be controlled by them.

Of course, there are some exceptional cases. Some speakers are wholly entranced, and some decarnate spirit asserts his personality, and carries it through while the soul of his instrument is being entertained else-where. And sometimes when no special claim is made certain persons in the audience recognize a personality by his manner, his diction, his spirit, and his lines of thought. But the more perfectly this takes place, the less does the medium know about it. I have myself had persons in the audience recognize some spirit who had inspired me. But invariably when this took place, nothing was in my mind but what I was speaking of. And in the thousands of times that I have spoken in public, I never once have thought of any spirits assisting me, but my mind has been wholly on the subject in hand.

We are all different ; there is no set rule. The main thing is to be sincere, and to have our whole being set on reaching the souls in the audience who need our help. It is thus, unless we be wholly entranced ; in this case some one else does the work, and the soul of the speaker is elsewhere. Of course, the value of what is said depends on the mental ability and the spirituality of the controlling spirit which is, however, limited in expression by the extent of those qualities possessed by the medium.

Yours for humanity and for spirituality.

LETTER THIRTY-FOUR.

The Worship of Jesus.

August 28, 1898.

To the Editor of THE BANNER OF LIGHT:

I was baptized into the Calvinistic Baptist Church, on my confession of faith, in December, 1852, and have therefore had from first to last considerable experience with the workings of orthodoxy. During these years I have noted a change in the attitude of the church towards Jesus.

In those early years, while they accepted in general the deity of Jesus and the atonement, they still sang in the hymns, and heard in the sermons and prayers, much of God. Jesus was the way to get to God, and his sacrifice made it possible for God to accept the repentant. But for the last twenty-five years the various branches of the evangelical church have gradually sunk, and are now engulfed in what I will call Jesusolatry. Old hymns, expressing worship of God, have been altered so as to make the worship paid to Jesus alone. And new stanzas have been incorporated into the body of devout hymns, bringing in the Jesus idolatry.

For instance, at a prayer-meeting the other night, after hearing them sing several hymns which rang the accustomed changes on Jesus, Jesus, nothing but Jesus, the pastor gave out " Home of the Soul," and I prepared to join in with alacrity. This poem had originally three stanzas. We sang two, and then I came to a new one incorporated by the Jesusolaters, and I closed the book in despair. They sang this new third and omitted the beautiful fourth, which closes with the line :

" To meet one another again."

And when I get up to speak, though I try to keep to the points on which we agree, for courtesy prevents me from actually proclaiming Spiritualism by name in a

Calvinistic meeting, yet I feel that they find in my remarks a sad want of the Jesus worship. Still, they
listen to me, and I would rather speak under some re-
strictions than not speak at all; for one can drop a seed
here and there that will take root in some hearts.

It is presumable that Moody has had more to do with
introducing this Jesus cult, to the sad neglect of the
two other members of the trinity, than any other one
man. At any rate, the Gospel Hymns carry out this
thought *ad nauseam*. As to the Christian Endeavorers,
they are fairly swamped and swallowed up—heart and
soul, body and bones—in this worship of a man. Of
course they would accuse us of blasphemy in return for
our accusing them of idolatry.

Not that we have anything against Jesus; so far from
that, we find a practical purity, a humanity, and a
spirituality in his recorded precepts that we fail to find
in those of Buddha, Confucius, and Mohammed. The
Golden Rule of Jesus is far superior to that of Confucius. The latter endorsed the negative remark of
one of his disciples that what he did not want to have
done to himself, he would not do to another, while the
precept of Jesus was to do to others what we *would* that
they should do to us. The Chinese teaching is not to
do harm to any one, while that of the Nazarene was to
show an active and an aggressive love to all with whom
we came in common contact. Kong-fu-tse was great,
but Jesus was higher.

Mohammed was about as far advanced in humanity
and spirituality as Moses. Buddha inculcated and practiced extreme purity and self-denial, but we find a more
lofty ideal in " what Jesus really taught." Or, if he was
not the one who taught thus, somebody did, and the
ideal is the same.

In the record of his words and ways we find that he
loved little children dearly, taking them in his arms
and blessing them, and bidding his less advanced disciples to be as teachable and simple as those little
children. It was he who praised the Samaritan because he tenderly and generously cared for the robbed

and wounded stranger. It was he who forgave those who put him to extreme physical torture by nailing his hands and feet to a cross, and then setting the cross up, letting the whole weight of his body come on the raw wounds. It was he who went afoot everywhere, curing the diseases of hundreds of sufferers without money and without price, not forgetting to inculcate right living and right feeling in the future.

It was he who stood and taught and healed day after day; and when his physical strength was all gone, went alone to some wild place to commune with nature and to be recuperated by decarnate spirits. It was he who rebuked the proud Pharisee, and praised the widow who contributed her little savings. It was he who preached the unparalleled Sermon on the Mount.

It opens with his analysis of those who are truly blest by the higher powers, and tells men to be just as perfect as the being whom he called his Father in heaven. In this superb discourse on right actions he declares that true morality is of the heart; that to be angry with any one is just the same as murdering him; that he who has an impure thought has committed an impure act; that righteousness is more important than clothing and food; and that goodness depends on our striving for it. He would have smiled sadly at the notion that any persons could use *his* goodness instead of their own.

Jesus was not perfect. He made some mistakes in word and deed that may be accounted for by his being a reformer and a radical, as well as a celibate. Supposing he did curse the fig tree. That fig tree had not borne a single fig for three years, and it was about time to cut it down. As to the tree's being withered up from the roots by his words, if that had been done by one of our mediums it would have been called a wonderful " test."

All this was the Jesus of the Gospel, and far more than we have space to declare. But the mistake of the church is in following the divine glamor of John, who looked in his old age at this pure, spiritual, and yet aggressive man as deity incarnate; and in being guided by the mistake of Paul, who claimed that any one can appropriate to himself the goodness of Jesus. These two fundamental errors have been like noxious weeds that have grown and spread in the garden of the church until they have almost killed the beautiful plants, heart-morality and worship of God alone.

We are sorry indeed that in this age of advancement so many in the churches should cling tenaciously to these fundamental errors, and that men like Moody and the leaders of the Endeavorers should inculcate so industriously what reason shows to be wrong. In fact, human reason, which springs from and allies us with infinite intelligence, they declare should not be used at all in matters of religion.

An intelligent observation of the trend of human affairs shows that acts must produce an actual effect on us and our posterity which cannot be effaced by any act of faith. And true religion binds every finite soul, consciously or unconsciously, to its infinite soul-parent without the intervention of any mediator. And religion is brought into action by striving to enter in at the straight gate, and walk in the narrow path of soul morality. Thus shall we tread the uplands of the path of the soul, and have for our companions those who seek the same ideal of perfection.

Yours for humanity and for spirituality.

LETTER THIRTY-FIVE.

Diet versus Drugs.

September 4, 1898.

To the Editor of THE BANNER OF LIGHT:

" A sound mind in a sound body," is a terse statement that has been prized for thousands of years, but it is one that impresses the average human being less in youth than with advancing years. The young quote it flippantly in their school essays : those who feel their physical powers waning ponder deeply on ways and means to make the body healthful.

As Spiritualists we are theoretically opposed to drugs. Drugs have come into use to nullify, or at least to lessen, the effect of some violation of the laws of nature.

A person has eaten too much improper food. He does this for a time with impunity, but at last the abused digestive organs mutiny against their lord and master, and raise such a commotion that the whole body is ill and nauseated. Then the drug man is summoned, and orders a dose. If he ordered ten times as much the patient would die, for these drugs are, as a general thing, virulent poisons. But as the amount of poison prescribed is small, the digestive organs set to work to expel it from the system. In getting rid of the poison, they incidentally get rid also of that improper food that was clogging the way, and it is devoutly believed by the patient that it was the medicine that made the cure. Having done so well one time, he continues to eat too much of improper food, because he thinks medicine will cure him again. By and by he does it once too often, and then a chronic inflammation of the digestive organs sets in, and he wonders why he should be so afflicted.

But if a person *will* indulge himself in wrong foods, he has to take drugs, and of course the sensible way is to avoid all that is improper in general, as well as those special articles of diet that heighten the particular tendency to disease to which his body is prone. It is all folly to say with the Christian scientist, " Nothing I eat can hurt me, if I only *think* that it cannot hurt me; " or, with a presumptuous Spiritualist, "Oh, I can eat what I am a mind to ; my spirit-friends will take care of that."

Merciful heavens ! have spirits nothing better to do than to labor to undo the effects of intemperance and gluttony ?

Certain persons have written me inquiries as to my statement in Letter Twenty-five regarding special articles of food that I am led to avoid. In that letter I said that if I " keep quiet, eat onions daily and avoid pie, cake, preserves, fat, strawberries, asparagus, tomatoes and beets, I sleep well and feel tolerably well."

Some of these foods should be avoided generally by all persons. These are pie, cake, preserves and coffee. Coffee affects the nerves and also makes one bilious. Fat should be eaten sparingly by all, for large quantities overwork the pancreas. It is not able to make a digestible emulsion of so much fat, the rest of its work falls on the already overworked liver, and biliousness is the result,

Pure milk, or sterilized milk, can be used generally, according to the idiosyncracies of one's own constitution.

As to sugar, strawberries, tomatoes, asparagus and beets, I avoid them conscientiously on personal grounds, · because of a tendency to too much uric acid in the system, and these articles tend to make that acid. Some uric acid in the body is all right, and some persons can use these articles without harm, but it would be the height of folly for one who had a tendency to too much of this acid to use the very foods that make it. For reasons connected with this condition I avoid starchy food, as potatoes and rice.

For the reasons stated above tomatoes are extremely bad for rheumatism, for that is a symptom of too much uric acid. I know a good old Baptist of seventy-five,

who is a martyr to rheumatism, and who eats tomatoes
at every meal, if possible, for two months in the summer. I have told him about it, and begged him to discard them ; but he is far too orthodox for that, and
considers his rheumatism as a direct dispensation of
Divine Providence. When I meet him, I ask him how
his rheumatism is. He tells me it is very bad. I tell
him that I am so sorry. He looks at me reprovingly
and piously remarks : "It is all right." He actually
thinks that it is the will of a personal God that he
should have rheumatism.

I am here reminded of one of my neighbors, who was
brought up a Roman Catholic, but has joined the Salvation Army. She calls herself a "holy ghost woman,"
whatever that may mean. She is a widow, and works
very hard to support her three children, who also work
industriously. They are all diseased. The boy of fourteen has a third abscess coming on his arm, and has
two on his leg. He is always having abscesses, and is
patient and sweet. The mother provides pork, and
none of them pay the slightest regard to what they eat.
She thinks that all these diseases come from the hand
of the Lord, are his will, and that their only duty is to
bow in meek submission to his high behests. One look
at this good woman showed me that she ought never to
have been married at all. She has a scrofulous neck.
It is no wonder that her offspring should have a heri-
tage of pain. She is very much alarmed about me,
because I have "rejected the only way of salvation."

We are glad that an anti-vaccination compromise bill .
has passed both the House of Commons and the House
of Lords. By this bill no child is required to be vacci-
nated before it is four years old; neither will it be
required after that age if the parent "specifies to the
court that he conscientiously believes that vaccination
would be prejudicial to the health of the child." So
parents in England can now save their children if they
are enlightened on the subject and have the resolution
to assert their right. "For this relief, much thanks."

Yours for humanity and for spirituality.

LETTER THIRTY-SIX.

The Czar's Proposal for Disarmament.

September 11, 1898.

To the Editor of THE BANNER OF LIGHT :

When Virgil led Dante down, ever down, through the nine circles of the terrible " Inferno," each successive circle imprisoning worse criminals who were subjected to yet more awful torture, on reaching the boundary of the eighth they were confronted by a yawning abyss, in the very bottom of which the traitors were confined and tormented in the sea of ice.

Clear around this abyss were massive stone turrets, in each of which a giant was chained. So large were they that though their feet rested in the ninth circle, their head and shoulders rose into the horrid eighth. By one of these the two explorers were at the command of Virgil taken in his hand and set down into the dread ninth, the region of cold, whose chill was intensified by the wings of Lucifer, who fanned this valley of the shadow of death with his mighty wings.

Chained with fetters that even they could not rend, each walled in by massive stone-work, on the very bottom of hell, these giants were penned; and securely fastened did Nimrod, Ephialtes, Typhon, and many more expiate their rebellion against the tyranical gods of their day and generation, according to the frightful creed of Dante and the Christian church in the thirteenth century.

Such a chained giant have the past centuries seen on the northern front of Europe and Asia. This penned-up giant is Russia. To the north are the frozen circum polar seas, and his only seaport there is Archangel, walled in by ice for nine months in the year. To the west are European powers who forbid him to advance one inch in their direction, and it was not till 1703 that Peter the Great seized enough land on the innermost corner of the Gulf of Finland to build Petersburg. To the south are strong powers who already occupied the land, and our century has seen him fight England and France combined, to secure a harbor for his ships on the great inland Black Sea.

To the south of his Asiatic possessions stands England, ever ready to menace his advance in that direction, and the mountain passes of Afghanistan have seen as bloody encounters as any in modern history. And to the east this struggling giant finds China barring his way except on the mountain-locked shores of Okhotsk and the cold, inhospitable confines of Behring Sea.

Besides these actual physical fetters and massive walls, our giant still labors under the effects of his subjugation by Tartary under Oktai. This slavery to the Mongols continued for two centuries, and is considered to be one of the many reasons why Russia has been at least two hundred years behind the rest of Europe.

Many have thought with indignation of this power for daring to exist at all on the edge of civilized Europe, with contempt for the uncivilized boors of the interior, and with helpless rage at the sufferings inflicted on Siberian exiles by a pampered and a tyrannical government.

But in the passage of years this Russian giant has struggled, not only for more sea coast where he could disport a navy like more favored nations, but also in the course of his evolution for more freedom and more light for his people. And every step that he has taken for enlightenment was received with astonishment by the other nations, who said with all the skepticism and rancor of the Jews of old, "Can any good thing come out of Russia ?"

When Alexander II. came to the throne in 1855, he made many reforms, the first of which was the abolition of serfdom. He established trial by jury, lessened the time of military service, and made other improvements. But when the poor Poles tried again for freedom they

were treated most severely, and eighty-five thousand
were transported to Siberia. Russian lovers of freedom could never pardon the government for the sufferings of these exiles, and the same year that saw Gar-
field assassinated, beheld the murder of Alexander II.
by an explosion of a bomb. It was a sad reward for
one who had done so much for his people; but this
people were like a wounded animal, who realizes his
pains, but does not always know just who is responsible
for them.

Later Czars have tried to make one language prevail
all through Russia, and probably but few outside of
her territory realize the amount of progress that has
taken place during the latter half of the nineteenth
century in this immense country, once the pity and the
scorn of western Europe.

But it is for us who dwell on the planet in 1898 to
be astonished and profoundly gratified by the proposal
made by the present Czar to the European powers in
favor of a provision for peace. He proposes, not a
complete disarmament, but a lessening of armament, so
as to make the taxes less severe, and allow the money
and labor spent for war to be used to advance the
nations in the arts of peace.

Though Nicholas II. has not gone so far as to pro-
pose the total abolition of war, yet he has gone immensely further than any other one has thought to go.
The strange part of the matter is that it was not Gladstone who might have thus put the crown to a noble
life who did this thing. It was not the President of
our own country. But it was the autocratic head and
front of the most autocratic government of Christendom that has taken the step. And a most auspicious
fact is the affable way in which most of the powers
have received this proposal. Had some other astute
power played this hand, he might have been accused
of insincerity and self-interest. But when Russia, occu-
pying in civilization and enlightenment the lowest
bench in the great school of nations, Russia, who has
most earnestly battled to get away some of the advant-

ages from more favored nations—when Russia makes
this proposal, all say: "Well, he is surely sincere, and
let us join in, and have an earnest consultation on this
matter."

I saw in one paper that France objects to disarmament until she has won back Alsace and Lorraine. Pray
Heaven that we shall not have to wait for that, for
France will *never* rule to the Rhine unless Germany be
annihilated, and France cannot annihiliate Germany. No,
no: we are very sorry for France, and realize how try-
ing it must be to give up the provinces and a billion of
dollars to her triumphant antagonist; but things are
as they are, and Celts must not expect to get the better
of Goths.

We were greatly pleased, Mr. Editor, with your edi-
torial on this proposal by the Czar in your issue of Sept.
10. The very least that can be said of the event is that
it is the first great official step towards universal peace.

When Alexander II. emancipated twenty-three million serfs in 1861, and when Lincoln's Emancipation
Proclamation took effect on Jan. 1, 1863, the State
papers that effected these events were of very great
importance. But to our mind this paper by the Czar is
greater than those, for this reason. Those acts related
to the interests of a single nation; while this new paper,
couched so modestly, as a mere suggestion, relates to
the interests of all the civilized world.

You alluded, Mr. Editor, in the article just adverted
to, to the fact that the present Czar is known to be an
earnest and sincere Spiritualist, and the strong proba-
bility that he was spirit guided to this act. It is well
known that Alexander II. emancipated the serfs under
the guidance of the spirit world; and still better known
that the great arisen fathers of this country gave Lincoln no peace until he had signed the paper giving
liberty to four million African slaves, held in bondage
by the laws of free America.

We congratulate the Czar that he is amenable to
spirit-influence in so noble a way. Many of the
crowned heads of European nations are said to be

Spiritualists. No doubt they accept the fact of spirit-return, but they have not always acted as nobly as has Nicholas. It was reserved for this ruler of a remote nation to listen to the voices that spoke the wisdom of the heavenly councils where sit the great founders and leaders of all nations, and to take the initiatory step that will no doubt lead eventually to a universal peace. The world can then progress as never before.

War is a survival of the early brutish and savage nature of man. He had to go through that condition in his gradual evolution from primitive man to seraph ; but it is time to leave that step of the ladder below and behind him, and mount to those regions where comprehended and accepted justice reigns.

Yours for humanity and for spirituality.

LETTER THIRTY-SEVEN.

The Troubles of Some Investigators.

September 18, 1898.

To the Editor of THE BANNER OF LIGHT:

One of the stumbling-blocks in the way of those who investigate Spiritualism is the fact that spirits give conflicting statements, not only concerning spiritual philosophy, but even in regard to modes of existence in spirit-life. These contradictions puzzle not only the new beginner, but even those who call themselves old-time Spiritualists.

The contradictions in philosophy arise from the fact that spirits are finite as well as mortals, and from the biases caused by early teachings and hereditary conditions, from which the disembodied have not yet been able to free themselves. The opposing statements regarding the modes of life beyond arise from the fact that the spirit-world of the earth is inconceivably large, and it is impossible for the most discursive spirit to know all about every part of it.

Some time ago, I received a letter from a man who had been plunged metaphorically into hot water, because recent investigations had proved conclusively that some of the phenomena which had been credited to the disembodied alone were sometimes accomplished by spirits yet in the flesh. He accused those who stated this to be a fact of not realizing the full significance of such a statement, and of putting a weapon into the hands of our opponents.

Such a state of mind as was evinced by this man interferes with the efforts of those who feel that the absolute truth should be forever the object of all our quests. We subscribe reverently and with all our hearts to these words from M. Gaston of Paris: "The truth for itself, without any regard to the consequences that may come in its train, be they good or bad, fortunate or to be regretted." Besides, the fear lest truth should overthrow spirit-return looks as if the one who fears is not quite sure that spirit-return is founded on truth. So sure are we, however, that it is a fact in nature that we court the fullest investigation, and are not afraid to go where actual facts learned by earnest search may lead ns.

The mental attitude of Spiritualists like the one alluded to above has fought the labors of the Society for Psychical Research. That society has, however, held the respect of thinkers at large ; and the frank avowal of Richard Hodgson, that many of the communicators are disembodied spirits, will have the more profound effect because he has in his long quest used all his ingenuity to account for every manifestation on some other hypothesis than the spiritualistic.

The person alluded to above also said in his letter that the spirits knew about as much about the next world as the preachers did, which was just nothing at all. He founded this assumption regarding the ignorance of the spirits—an extraordinary assumption on the part of of a professed Spiritualist—on the fact that entranced mediums often give contradictory statements. He gave as examples the opposing statements regarding re-incarnation and the existence of animals in the spirit-world.

He seems to think that as soon as persons get out of the body, they at once all believe the same on philosophical points, go to just the same place, and see precisely the same things. He does not realize that mental range and modes of existence to the disembodied are just as varied as on the earth-plane. In fact, they are as much more varied as the spirit world of the earth is more extensive than the six-foot layer of space that follows the configurations and the convolutions of the planet, where the embodied breathe.

The entrancing spirit of one medium teaches re-incarnation, or that Jesus was the god of this planet, and made it, because he is taught these things by higher spirits, who oppose those who teach otherwise on the convenient hypothesis that those who differ from them are not yet advanced enough to dwell where they dwell. The controlling spirit of another medium teaches that we are not re-incarnated and that we progress, always in more ethereal bodies, that respond to a higher scale of vibrations, after once quitting the fleshly integument; and that Jesus was a Jew and a finite man. All this does not prove that disembodied spirits have no existence. It simply shows that all controlling spirits do not have the same experiences, and that their theories regarding what they have not seen and felt are just as varied as when they dwelt on the earth-plane.

The man of the letter said, with regard to one spirit's saying that animals dwell in the spirit-world, while another declares the contrary, that this was not a matter of *opinion*, but of *fact*. He illustrated by saying that if we went to Florida, we might disagree as to the effect the climate has on a certain disease, but we would all agree that oranges grow there.

His position illustrates what was said in the early part of this letter about the spirit-world being inconceivably large, thus presenting in its different parts

much variety in the modes of existence. We are tempted
to enquire how large he thinks the spirit-world is. We
must try our hand at an illustration to match the one
he used.

Suppose that people lived on the moon, and that a
man who has always lived in Florida goes to the moon
and tells them about the lakes and the luxuriant vege-
tation and sweet golden fruit to be found where he came
from. Then suppose that a man who has always lived
in Iceland goes to the moon and tells about the lava
tracts and the glaciers. When they ask about the
juicy oranges, he laughs them to scorn and says he
never saw such a thing in his life. The lunar people
think that these men have never been to the earth at
all, or that they are arrant liars. So they feel till a
wise man arises and says the earth is very large and
perhaps has many climates and modes of existence.

We are now in the habit of thinking John's heaven, a
cube measuring fifteen hundred miles square, a rather
boxed-up affair. But Florida has not the superficies of the
bottom layer of John's heaven. Our spirit-world is immense, in its lowest layer extending over the whole
superficies of the earth, but expanding in every direction far beyond the distance of the moon. Doubtless
animals continue to live in its lowest sphere, in the part
close to the place in earth where they once dwelt;
while some who are psychologically held to human
beings accompany for a time to regions beyond. One
spirit hates an animal, never sees one, and does not
intend to lie when he says there are none at all in the
spirit-world. Another spirit loves these beings lower
than himself, rejoices at their exemption from the sufferings of earth, and is attended by troops of highly
developed cats, loving dogs, and faithful horses. He
comes back and says there are animals in the spirit-
world. And so there are, in his part of it. And I am
free to confess that I like the nature of this second
spirit better than the first. Supposing high spirits did
not love us, because we are less advanced than they!

The summer before I found out that Spiritualism
was true, my dog, who had been so devoted to me for
four and a half years, was killed by burglars, who got
into the house the fourth night after. He died for
those he loved. I remember saying later to my friends
that I must be in a very low state. I said all the heaven
I wanted was a beautiful grassy place shaded by trees.
I would be sitting upon a little knoll with my dog by my
side, and my friends who walked in the road below
would look up and say, "There's Miss Judson and
Nicky."

Yes: there is a love commingled with reverence that
we feel toward those who are higher, wiser, and better
than we are. And there is a love commingled with
compassion because of their limitations—"straitened,"
as dear Mrs. Browning said of her little "Flush"—
which we feel to those who are lower than we, and can
protect from harm. We want to feel both these kinds
of love, as well as the equal love and companionship we feel for our peers. Then our love nature, link-
ing us as it does to our infinite and divine source, is
developed in every direction, and becomes the ladder
by which we can rise to greater heights.

Yours for humanity and for spirituality.

LETTER THIRTY-EIGHT.

Organization.

September 25, 1898.

To the Editor of THE BANNER OF LIGHT:

While sitting last evening for spirit communion and
instruction, I was suddenly startled and delighted to see
my father's face close to me on my positive side. He
looked very bright and earnest, and my mental attitude
was as always when directly conscious of his presence,
that of "Speak, for your daughter hears."

No more came then, and I spent the rest of the evening doing nothing in particular, and retired early, feeling quite sleepy. When nearly asleep, I began to think on a subject that has not specially engaged my attention. The thoughts came fast, and I will reproduce them in this letter, merely adding that when I see a spirit, followed by an influx of thoughts, I am assured that they come from that spirit, especially when they accord with his line of interest. In general it makes me sleepless to think my own thoughts after retiring. But when a spirit psychologizes me to the extent of giving me thoughts, I at once go to sleep after they have ceased to flow in, and awake in the morning with the same impressed upon my brain.

Is organization desirable? The answer to this question depends wholly on what organization really is, and whether the thing alluded to accords with the true meaning. What it really is is to be found in our invaluable companion, the unabridged dictionary.

An organ is an instrument by which an action is performed. An organized body is made up of several different organs, which cohere into a whole, while each one of them performs its own function. Organization is the act of organizing, or the state of being organized. Coleridge said, "What is organization but the connection of parts in and for a whole, so that each part is at once end and means?" We accept these definitions, illustrated as they are by the poet-philosopher, "S. T. C."

According to this, if an organ has its own function, and if one man can do his part well only when all his organs work diligently and harmoniously, then it is only by organization that many men can work effectually toward a common end. This being so *prima facie*, it only remains for us Spiritualists to organize truly, so that we may accomplish the end that we desire.

To illustrate a great error and a great truth in the mode of procedure, we will speak of the organization of the Society of Jesus and the government of the United States.

In the former case organization exists, for from the general down to the lowest postulant each member knows where he belongs, and has his own work to do. The general presides over four classes or members, and each class has its own department of work. The professed have been through all the stages, have taken all the vows, and are able to elect a new general, if needed, but only from their own grade. The coadjutors assist the professed. The scholastics devote themselves to study and to teaching. The novices are preparing for higher work. The work designed is accomplished. The flaws are that the system works like a wheel within a wheel, excluding new and fresh blood; and that absolute obedience is enforced on each inferior by the one next superior to him.

It is said that the inferior need not obey when the superior commands what is sinful. But as it is the general alone who decides what is sinful, and as the inferior who objects runs great risks, we see that the Society of Jesus is really a small papacy. Such a kind of organization Spiritualists do not want.

The Constitution of the United States is ideally gotten up, and only needs to be lived up to to work out perfection. The three departments—the legislative, judicial and executive—have their own functions, and yet they play into each other just enough to prevent each one from becoming too rigid. The members of all the departments, from the President down, are chosen, directly or indirectly, by all the people, with the exception of minors, the insane, paupers, women and idiots. With the exception of the disability of women, the government is planned to be truly representative. To be so, each officer is actually elected by those who are proved to be competent to elect him. It would not do for any smart man who had a number of devoted friends to say, "Well, let us send a representative to the House in Washington to work for our interests." No, no; our representatives must be actually chosen, each by the proper quota of the population of his own State. If otherwise, the representative character of the government of our country would be flawed.

We, as Spiritualists, in organizing nationally for the Cause we hold so dear. need to be guided by the principles and the example (when constitutional) of our own country. To give the acts of this body weight, it should be truly representative. To make it actually representative, each delegate should be chosen by an actually existing, chartered, and *organized* body in the section from which he comes. Just as no representative can sit in Congress unless he has been actually elected in the ways provided by the Constitution, so no delegate should be allowed to sit in the deliberative sittings of the N. S. A. unless he has been actually chosen by an *actually organized* society. Just as no representative to the United States Government can be sent by any chance association of individuals, so should no delegate be sent to represent anything but a *bona fide* organized body. If our National Association be made up of properly elected delegates, the question then becomes, "Who are bound to be guided by the acts of this representative body? Are all the Spiritualists in the United States thus bound?"

It is clear that only those Spiritualists are thus bound, and especially assisted in their local work, who belong to a local organized body, a majority of whom have elected a delegate to the National Assembly.

Many Spiritualist meetings are carried on by one medium. He hires a hall, and appoints a doorkeeper, who sells our papers, and takes the dime admission fee. This fee is called a "silver collection" in some places. As our smallest silver coin is a dime, those who come know that is the admission fee. The medium takes care of the platform, and asks whom he chooses to assist him, or does all the work, if he so prefer. He appoints circles during the week. All the money cleared goes into his own pocket. He is responsible to no one, as he hires the hall himself. There were many such meetings held last winter. They are not societies, they have no right to a charter, nor to membership with the National Spiritualists Association, nor to send delegates to it.

To uphold our Cause, Spiritualists should organize for work everywhere, and not leave it all to a medium, whether test or speaker, who does it for a living. They should organize, whether they hold Sunday meetings in a hall or not. They can organize as Spiritualists, have their officers and by-laws, and meet regularly in a hall or in each others' houses. Such associations would be entitled to charters, membership with the N. S. A., and to send a delegate. They could work in any direction they chose: Sunday evening meetings, aiding the poor, humane work, a free reading-room, or for social purposes. Conducted by earnest Spiritualists, who work to advance humanity and spirituality, and not for the money in it, they would become influential in the community, and thus unite with many grand spiritualistic societies in the country to strengthen the hands of the National Association, and to further the extension of our glorious, our angelic Cause.

Yours for humanity and for spirituality.

LETTER THIRTY-NINE.

Belief in God.

October 2, 1898.

To the Editor of THE BANNER OF LIGHT:

Many Spiritualists declare that they do not believe in God. This is owing to their natural recoil from the notion of God, brought to a head, as it were, by John Calvin. That conception of God is of a hateful and hate-awakening being who uses his supernatural power to damn a race already cursed by his own want of foresight, unless they accept a way of deliverance which militates against every spark of manhood, is productive of immorality, and contradicts every principle of justice. They can accept this one way of salvation, provided they have been elected to do so. If they have been so elected, it is only God that they will praise through eternity; if they have not been so elected, they will have only themselves to blame, as they writhe in the torments of the lost forever and ever.

Many taught thus were so terrified by this monstrosity, and are later so disgusted by it, that they say there is no God at all, and perhaps add that all the God there is is man himself. But let us see.

All mankind, after ascending from the brute have had a notion of a free and conscious intelligence. They conceive a superior mind back of and beyond all that they perceive with their senses, which sets the forces of nature at work. No matter how imbruted the people may have been they have believed thus. Or rather, instead of believing thus, they have known it intuitively. At first, they knew it dimly and unconsciously. As the race developed they knew it more clearly. With this knowledge there was always an intuition that between this Master Mind beyond and themselves there was a link. And this consciousness of a link between mortal man and the great intelligence which rules nature is the origin of all religion.

But just at this point there came in, sooner or later, with all races and peoples, a marring influence. This hurtful influence was that of the priest; and when the priesthood was organized, the influence became more corrupt.

Priests have arisen, not to teach man more and better about his personal relations with the unseen, for each can learn them better for himself. It is by following one heavenly intuition in one's own soul that one can gain another, and not by following the direction of some one else because he is a priest, or a clergyman, or a bishop, or a pastor, or an evangelist, or a Sunday-school teacher. But, among all people and in all ages, priests of some sort arose and claimed that they, and they alone, had all knowledge and all commands that divine intelligence wished to communicate to mortals.

The object of the priest was two-fold. One object was to have an assured and most comfortable means of support, and the other was to control mankind. They soon found that they could attain those objects more effectually by organizing into a hierarchy; and where they succeeded in combining what they called religion with the government, their power became still greater. The secular arm was combined with the arm of the church, and no one must speak a word against this double team, on pain of destruction.

Of course we realize and admit that there were always some humane and humble-minded priests who worked for the good of their charge, but these were in the minority, were laughed at by the worldly-wise ones, and were not able to assert themselves effectually, on the principle that devils "rush in where angels fear to tread."

Though Milton had a natural bias toward prelacy, he administered many scathing rebukes to the unfaithful guides who did not feed the sheep, and threatened them with that " two-handed engine " which stood ready " to smite once, and smite no more."

In all ages priests have *interfered* between the soul of man and God. In the old days, my mates and I could not be sure that we were Christians unless some minister should hear us relate the exercises of our minds, and tell us that we had gone safely through the door. To be really sure, we must relate them to the church at the convenant meeting, be probed by the questions of the senior deacons, and be voted to be worthy of membership while we were secluded in another room. After that we were baptized.

Never shall I forget my distress of mind the evening after I had gone through all this. I had related my experience to the church, had been accepted, had been baptized, and had partaken for the first time of the Lord's supper. Everybody told me I was all right, and yet unutterable gloom settled down on my soul, and

penetrated all its recesses that very night. That gloom
clung ever to me until I swung clear from all churches,
all priests, all creeds, all Bibles, and learned how

> " In secret silence of the mind,
> My heaven, and there, my God, to find."

The soul and God, that is enough. The intermed-
dling of any other soul is officious. A human being to
mediate between the soul and its Infinite parent is
folly. To make a human being into a mediator between
God and the whole of mankind, and then set him on a
throne by the side of God, is idolatry.

It is all this blasphemy, all this idolatry, all these
paraphernalia, all this attempt to bind the soul of man
in chains, by the fear of the church or the priest and
the desire to be and do like the rest, that have driven
some persons, otherwise intelligent, into atheism. If
any of us have sunk into that gulf, through the recoil
from the Jewish Jehovah or the God of Calvin, or the
tyranny of the priesthood, let us endeavor to rise therefrom.

An old Hebrew medium said it was only the fool who
says there is no God, and in that day he only said it
only in his heart. Of course the tutelary spirits of
Abraham and Moses and Jesus are not God. Jesus made
a plain distinction (it seems plain to us) between
his father, his controlling spirit who was greater than he
was, and with whom he was one, and " God who is
spirit."

Many think with us that beings less than infinite
created worlds (—expressed on pages 128 and 129 of
" The Bridges Between Two Worlds ") and reason
makes us know that Infinite Intelligence is beyond all
such " gods " and " world builders," and just as far beyond as infinity goes beyond the finite. These finite
beings work according to the rules of geometry: the
infinite *is* geometry. The finite use already existing
atoms in their operations; the infinite expresses itself
eternally by an infinite number of atoms.

Mr. Dawbarn makes the clear-headed and rational statement that matter, force, and intelligence are all the universe; and that every single atom has the three in it. We wholly agree with him, and think moreover, that the intelligence in each and every atom is a portion of that infinite intelligence which deep and reverent souls acknowledge, whether the name employed be God, Allah, Jehovah, Oromasdes, Om, or Brahm.

After the invention of the telescope and the discovery of the Copernican laws had immensely widened the human outlook, a poet said, " the undevout astronomer is mad." In view of the psychological discoveries of the present century, which are after all but pigmy steps compared with the mighty strides that are to come, may we not say with still more truth, " the undevout philosopher is mad." The " half-gods " build worlds according to the mathematics that regulate the relations of worlds and of systems of worlds. To the infinite mind these relations that seem complicated to them are an open book. In a superb sense, " He is the form." Shall puny man fail to adore infinite intelligence ? He can stretch his intellect to the utmost in studying its works. Let him also use all his spiritual powers in unceasing adoration.

Yours for humanity and for spirituality.

LETTER FORTY.

My Morning Glories.

October 10, 1898.

To the Editor of THE BANNER OF LIGHT :

For many years it has made me sad to see the first golden rod swing its unique spray of little yellow bells. The sadness came because the appearance of the golden rod showed that summer was over, and the long, cold, dreary winter was not far away. Especially was it so with me in Minnesota, where the summers are shorter and fiercer and the winters longer and far colder than in New England. The golden rod seems less sad this year than in the past, probably because we must all rejoice that this peculiar summer is ended, and also because I found a winter in mild New Jersey less distressing than in high latitudes or along the Eastern sea coast.

But life must wane, or rather its manifestations decrease, as the season advances, and we are reminded of the beautiful name given to our home beyond "God's ether blue," the "Summerland."

Life is unending, and we think we are right in calling it the primal cause; but its manifestations are regulated by certain conditions. These conditions are of course light, air, moisture, and heat. If all these are provided, we have a beautiful world, unless we be penned up by city walls. If one of these conditions be wanting, animal and vegetable life is hampered, and what is hampered decreases in beauty.

In my back-yard many morning glories sprang up from seeds that were sown long before I came to live in New Jersey. I transplanted several, and placed them with others that had started beneath my study window. I did it because it seemed too bad to let the little darlings perish amid the thrifty weeds, not realiz-

ing how they would reward my care. I put in little
stakes, and fastened the strings above the cellar window. The puppy pulled up the stakes, and chewed up
the leaves, so I put a little chicken wire to ward off the
persistent and comical marauder.

They had plenty of air, water, sunlight, sunheat, and
something to cling to. They soon reached the top of
the cellar window, and put out long, tender, and altogether graceful shoots, and the strings were lengthened
to the study window. When they reached there they
began to bloom. The colors are royal purple, lavender,
red, pink, and white with delicate purple streaks in each
lobe, painted by nature's unerring pencil. On a bright
morning they are a mass of bloom, and even when the
glowing sun has shriveled their delicacy, the tender
green sprays of leafage deck the window without darkening it, and make me happy every time I look at them.

The honeysuckle is fragrant, but its mode of climb-
ing is less graceful than that of the morning glory. Its
positive stem turns from left to right, and each new
shoot stands out almost as rectangularly as that of a
baby-oak. But the morning glory turns from right to
left, and each shoot grows in a tender curve, that
makes it a thing of beauty and a joy forever. And,
except the bloom itself, what is prettier than the un-
opened bud?

Some object to morning glories that they are too
short-lived. They would not be so ethereally beautiful
if they lasted longer. Dahlias and gladioli out-last
them; but compare the sword-like stiffness of the leaves
and flower-spike of a gladiolus, and the coarse, flaunt-
ing, round dahlia, with the graceful shape, the delicate
bloom, and the evanescent transparency of the morning
glory.

In view from my kitchen window is another plant of
the same species. While getting breakfast I always
look to see the condition of its royal blooms, for this is
the rich purple. Though but one plant, it looks like
ten, and I have seen more than thirty "glories" at
once.

This one sowed itself at the root of an old stump. I disregarded it at first, and the puppy trod it down as if it were the stubble of the field. But it would grow and threw out so many thrifty shoots that I put a nail in the stump, and tied a strong cord to the top of the clothes-pole. All the shoots went up it, twisted in wild confusion together, and the sag of the rope gives such a graceful curve to the whole mass. I watered it occasionally, and the next I knew was the admiration of the neighbors for that beautiful morning glory.

The shoots at the top of the clothes-pole have nothing to cling to, and have thrown themselves out in the most happy-go-lucky manner. But this morning I was amazed to see a number of shoots twisted together, and the whole pointing straight up to the sky. It did not sway at all, and I thought of looking about the yard for a yogi, and a rope coming down moored fast to some sure support in the sky. But I saw no yogi, and sat looking and wondering to see it stand so straight.

After a l'ttle the delicate top began to sway and to curl, and later the whole mass gracefully bent, as if it were tired of holding up so long. Their almost human succumbing to physical weakness makes me think of a scene in Faust which I saw in Germany in 1877. The whole of the play was presented, for the first time since Goethe wrote it, in Leipsic the year before; and, fortunately for me, it was reproduced in Hanover during the three months I spent there. The scene the weary morning glories make me think of is this:

Mephistopheles made a beautiful vision appear before the eyes of the sleeping Faust. Some twenty little girls stood on a pyramid of flowers, clasping each other's hands. On the very point of the pyramid stood a lovely little three-year-old child, with her arms stretched upwards. The audience was in an ecstacy. The children were so motionless that I for one could not tell whether they were real or made of wax. It was encored, and yet again did we drink in its beauty. The third time, just before the curtain fell, I saw the tired arms of the topmost tot droop; and then I knew that it was some German mother's darling, who should have been sleeping in her crib several hours before.

I think that early this morning these morning glory shoots got so tired of looking for something to cling to, that they made a league together that they would hold each other up, if there was no other way. Each one said: "If you will hold me up, I will hold you up." And so the six made out to stand up straight towards the clear blue sky. But, like the little German child, they are tired now and are bending down, but altogether, and of course all twisted the same way.

Alive! Of course they are alive. If they were not, we should not have them in the spirit-land. And they feel pain from a rough grasp, and a worse pain when rudely torn from the parent stem.

One dewy morning I took an early walk in the suburbs of Worcester. I came to a by-path, and there lay a quantity of flowers that had been torn from some flowering tree. The branches had been roughly broken, and the hands that did the deed belonged to vandals who did not want the flowers. They broke them off and dashed them to the ground. I felt so sorry for them, and for the maimed parent tree. I could not restore them and make them live again; but I took each spray up tenderly and laid it in the dewy grass, where it would not be trodden on, and where its life could pass out peacefully.

I think we ought to teach children not to pluck flowers too ruthlessly. They should learn to pluck them carefully, and only those that they really want to carry to mamma, who was too busy to walk with them, to the sick playmate or feeble and aged friend, or to deck the tea table and make the sitting room look pretty for papa when he comes home tired. They should learn not to seize them in masses and then throw them away.

I suppose when this letter is done I shall put the ladder against the roof of the back porch, and rig a cord from the top of the clothes pole to the corner of the roof, so that these aspiring and well-nigh discouraged morning glories can still climb. By the time they reach the roof of the porch the frost will come, and these present flowers will bloom in spirit-land, for the happy children there, and their little seeds will give us new blooming plants after the winter has passed away.

Yours for humanity and for spirituality.

LETTER FORTY-ONE.

" Our Ancestors."

October 14, 1898.

To the Editor of THE BANNER OF LIGHT:

Some of our readers may be familiar with John P. Cooke's very spiritual brochures entitled "God" and "The Only God." The title page of the latter bears two pictures called "Whence" and "Whither." The first represents the primitive man and woman sheltered in a forest. The second shows two forms rising from a rocky coast by a wide ocean on mother earth. The smaller form is a just arisen spirit, who stretches one hand toward the glory beyond on which his gaze is fixed. He is borne upward by a strong angel whose feet have just left the rocky coast. Both forms are bathed in light which comes down from the celestial realm. This picture is beautiful, and is similar to others that we have seen.

It is with the first picture, called "Whence," that we have to do to-day. It is a copy of a wonderful painting by Gabriel Max, entitled, "Our Ancestors." It impresses one deeply at the first glance, and the more one ponders it the more is he struck by the originality and the force of the artist's conception. We will try to describe it.

Sitting on the ground, with her face directly towards us, is this primitive woman, this Eve we may call her, as pictured in the latter part of the nineteenth century.

Her long, light hair, parted in the middle, falls an un-
tended mass upon her shoulders. Her lower limbs are
slightly crossed, and one sees at a glance the thumb-
like character of the great toe of the right foot. This
early woman of the primitive wilds used her feet for
grasping as well as her hands, when it suited her con-
venience to do so. Held in her arms, as she sits at
ease on the ground, is her infant. All we see of him
is his little back, which she tenderly holds, and a part
of one round arm. He is nursing, and, as with our
own babies at such a time, his mind holds no other
thought.

Let us now return to this woman's face. Her features are large and coarse, if compared with the spark-
ling American type or the rare delicacy of a beautiful
Pole. But it is not the face of an animal. Long, with
its noble forehead half hidden by the hair, it will develop into powerful beauty with a few thousand years.
In fact, some of our women a few years ago, with their
matted brush of hair covering the forehead to the very
eyebrows, looked more like animals than does this free-
born creature of the woods. Determination, foresight,
courage, are on her features. But it is in looking into
her intense and human eyes that we see her soul. Her
posture, her expression, her eyes, bespeak one thought,
it is this: "Nothing shall harm my little child." Let
danger come, and that form, alert in its ease, will be
electrified into violent and effective action; and the
fierce quadrupeds of the forest will slink away from this
mother at bay.

But this woman is not alone. There are two in this
interesting duet, and there are but two, for they are
monogamists; and though she may seem somewhat coarse
to the present civilization, yet it was for her delicacy,
for her "sweet, attractive grace," that she was chosen,
and perhaps fought for, by this powerful, primitive
man.

We see his face and his form in profile. For this
reason he seems at first more brutish than the woman.

She looks somewhat naked, excepting her hair. His skin is so toughened by exposure and hardships that it looks like a carefully-fitted hide. His abdomen protrudes, as if he had just broken most plentifully the fast of days. That is probably the case. These ancestors of ours did not have five meals a day, like the Germans; nor four meals a day like the English; nor even the American breakfast, dinner, and supper. They esteemed themselves fortunate if they had a good square meal in two or three days, with occasional lunches of a fish or a bird, and little tidbits thrown in of snails and locusts.

Our ancestors were not vegetarians, but meat-eaters. Their posterity made wild fruit delicious by cultivation; but while primitive man could stay his hunger, in case of necessity, on shoots of trees and acorns and other nuts, yet he craved flesh, and could not be content without it.

In our picture, this rough but faithful fellow realized that his mate was not quite so strong as usual, and was also impeded in the chase by the little one. So thought for her, as well as his own empty stomach, has led him to make an extra effort, and it was a young and a remarkably toothsome primitive cow that he caught and killed and dragged home; and by way of a condiment, he fell in with a litter of little boars, which he took the trouble to bring along.

They did not cook these creatures. Fricasseeing, roasting with truffles, the stew and even the plain broil were then unknown. They divided it as best they could with hands and feet, got at the flesh within the hair and the bristles, and hunger made a good sauce. And we may be sure that this rough fellow let his mate have the choicer bits, and did not quarrel with her if she intercepted a specially savory morsel, and put it into her own mouth. No doubt he thought to himself that she had to eat for two.

Look at him, now that they have eaten their fill and are ready to rest. They are in the depth of the forest,

and she has taken shelter by a fallen tree that rests
against some natural support. He is fearful that it
may slip and do her harm. She knows not what he is
doing. Her eyes look far away into space. Her only
thought is how she loves that little thing and how she
will kill anything that comes to hurt it. He pushes his
weight against the fallen tree, his brawny arm is raised
against it, his great hand pushes it, and he looks down
at his wife and child. Tenderness and protecting love
soften those rough features, that hide-like skin, that
massive frame.

How do you like this conception of those from whom
we sprung? It differs in almost every particular from
the one that was read to us in childhood from the second chapter of Genesis. This one is wholly natural,
that had the supernatural woven in. This one follows
the course of nature, which is a constant development
from lower to a little higher. That one made a perfect
man at one jump out of the dust of the ground, and a
woman out of a rib taken from the man's side. And
this unscientific mode of procedure has been accepted as
the truth for thousands and thousands of years. In
this one, the man and woman can scarcely talk, for
language is rudimentary at first, and develops as modes
of living and modes of thinking become more complex.
In that, Adam and Eve talked with inbred ease, and
even that bad snake, whom Goethe mischievously calls
" our auntie," can talk too. Goddess of reason, where
are we? Is this a fairy story for unreasoning three-year
olds, or is this supposed to be sacred history? And
God talked too, and with a voice that awoke corres-
ponding vibrations in the tympana of Adam's ears, and
God was walking in the garden in the cool of the day.
He was probably " materialized."

And how disgracefully and selfishly this perfect man
in the Bible, fresh from the hands of his Creator, be-
haved! He was quite ready to eat the apples which
Eve generously shared with him; and then, when he
found he was to be blamed for doing so, he lays it onto

her, and even hints that God himself is also to blame.
"The woman whom thou gavest to be with me, she
gave me, and I did eat!" Poor fellow! Differing from
some of the men of this generation, he did not dare to
refuse when it was offered to him. Well, they were all
punished severely, and even that remarkably endowed
snake was condemned to eat dust all the rest of his life.

We confess to liking Mr. Max's primitive man much
better than the one in "The Bible." Adam was supposed to be created perfect, and proved himself to
be a selfish coward. Primitive man in our picture
labored hard, protected his wife, did the best he knew
how in every way, and bequeathed his good qualities
to his descendants. Adam had everything done for
him, and had not sense enough to avoid doing the one
thing that his patron had told him not to do; his oldest
son became a murderer, while Abel put on the airs of a
saint and talked so aggravatingly to Cain that he was
killed for it. Adam's posterity turned out so badly
that God exterminated all of them by a flood except
the family of Noah, who was supposed to be saved on
account of his goodness, but acted so indecently that
we shall drop the subject on the spot.

God speaks to man, but not by such crude tales. The
all-inclusive Soul from which we sprung speaks to you,
to me, not by an audible voice, but by an influx of just
as much reason, wisdom and love as we are now fitted
to crave. This asking is not done by a direct appeal
to the infinite. It is done by emptying the soul of all
conflicting elements and opening it to heavenly influence. So asking, we shall receive.

Yours for humanity and for spirituality.

LETTER FORTY-TWO.

The Soul Expressed by the Physical Form.

October 21, 1898.

To the Editor of THE BANNER OF LIGHT ·

How is it that we often feel well acquainted with persons with whom we have never exchanged a word ? We meet them on the street, we do not know their names, nor where they live, and yet their inner nature is like an open book. Of one we say to overselves that here is one we can trust; and to him would we go to for aid if we were in sore need. Of another, we know he is bad, and we would deeply pity the little child who must call him father.

Culture and breeding, or their lack, become manifest in the way the words come from a person's lips; but the soul stands revealed, though no word be spoken, in the features themselves, though in repose. An artist sits within, and day by day, year by year, he does his work. Every thought, every feeling, every wish, chisels something on the plastic face and the form; and these little marks, so fine that they are individually invisible, reveal clearly to those who behold the lineaments, what manner of man or woman dwells within.

Many, especially the young, desire to be beautiful, and fancy that beauty lies solely in the tint and freshness of the skin, in the brightness of the eyes, in the abundance of the hair, in the regularity of the features, and in the grace and ease of the carriage. Yet we can all recall persons who did not possess these, who had more lovers of their own and of the opposite sex than those who were acknowledged to possess more beauty.

I well remember the attractive power possessed by a dear friend of my youth. Everybody, if forced to acknowledge the truth, said she was very "homely."

Her complexion was bad, her eyes were small, and of
no particular color, her mouth was large, and not well
shaped. Her nose was very large, and, so far from
having the dignity and character of a Roman, all one
could say of it was that it was a large nose. And yet
this girl had innumerable friends of both sexes, and
many ardent lovers who did their best to win her to
walk life's pathway by their side. The one she finally
married had loved her as long as Jacob sought Rachel
of old; and is a much nobler man than that old patri-
arch.

I had not seen my friend for many years. But a lecture engagement led me near her, and we eagerly
brightened the old links of friendship's chain. To my
delighted surprise, the homely girl of forty years ago
had become a very handsome old lady. A happy married life, and the love of good children, who repay her
fond care by their devotion, have made her face bloom
with happiness, and surely no one is loved more and ad-
mired than herself in the town where she lives. In her
is exemplified the truth that a loving, candid, and sym-
pathetic nature makes one more beautiful with advancing years.

So when I hear young people wish that they were
beautiful, I tell them that however plain they may think
themselves in youth, they may be sure of growing in
beauty as old age advances. And when to kindness of
heart is added the fine chiseling made by thought, to
which the spiritualized soul gives an indescribable and
a nameless grace, we have a face that the casual passer-
by looks at again and again, and longs to know. Even
the poor brute, tethered and hungry, feels a something
he knows not what in the gracious presence, and turns
his head, and follows with wishful eye, till such a one
be out of sight.

Which would one choose on the whole to be, as fair
as Helen of Troy in youth, and to deteriorate into a
querulous, selfish and loveless old age; or to be originally plain, and yet make one's self a beautiful old man

or woman by the transforming power of benevolence, unselfishness, and spiritual thought ? Edmund Spenser's fine lines are in point here:

> " For of the soul the body form doth take,
> For soul is form, and doth the body make."

We cannot, however, agree wholly with what is here expressed If he had said the soul *has* form or *takes* form, it would have been correct in our view. But we cannot think that soul *is* form. Soul is one thing; form and expression another. Soul is wholly immaterial. It is conscious, it is free; and it uses form of greater or less ethereality by which to express itself.

That the character moulds the face is shown by examining the features of babyhood. The mother feels that she can recognize her own infant, and select it from a multitude; though there are instances on record where she failed to do so. But to an outsider, little babies have no very distinguishing features. Of course one would not take a dark-eyed one for one with blue eyes, nor a light-haired one for a dark, nor the plump, well-cared-for pet for the pining, half-starved waif. They all have an innocent look, and when they smile they have the tranquil smile that the angels wear.

But as months and years roll on, there comes a change. The features of each one become individualized; and it could only be a very indifferent person who could take one four-year-old for another. The forehead develops with a growing intellect or is clouded by a sluggish brain; the eyes look brightly into our own, rove with unthinking gaze over distant objects, or sullenly seek the ground; the nose becomes a distinct feature; the mouth, little revealer of the inner character, is wreathed in loving smiles, is drawn down with discontent, or is closed firmly, showing the resolute and undaunted nature of the soul within. This process goes on year by year, until the skilful observer need only look at a person's face to know what manner of man he is.

The form, as well as the face, is a great revealer. I
had a friend who said she could tell the character of a
stranger by looking at his back while he was walking.
The gait, the mode of standing, the attitude while at
work, the voice, the penmanship, all—all tell the stuff
of which we are made within.

Look at the next aged person you see in the street car.
Study the features, note the atmosphere of him or her,
get into spiritual *rapport* with the person's inner nature.
And what you do to another, others will do to you; and,
though they may not know *who* you are, they can judge
unerringly *what* you are.

Our physical self thus becomes open to the searchings
of the physical eyes of others.   Still, wrong inferences
are sometimes drawn because of the complicated nature
of the being within, as well as from the clumsiness of
the flesh itself.   But the disembodied ones who walk
by our side make no mistakes.   They do not look at our
fleshly body, but with spirit-vision look at our spirit-
form.   Our fleeting thoughts, feelings, desires, and
resolutions are all expressed there.

It will be the same when we pass entirely out of the
fleshly body.   There will be no need of any further research, for the disembodied will see us as we are.   And
if we still delude ourselves in that new condition by
thinking that we are better, kinder, and wiser than we
are, we shall soon know our true status by seeing what
kind of spirits are attracted into the atmosphere which
has been formed about us by our acts while still in the
earthly body.

How sad it would be to find ourselves in the spirit-
world, and yet not fit to be a companion with the revered father, the idolized mother, or the precious little
child who left us long before and has grown up in the
society of angels !

But in such a case our sadness will give birth to our
longing to improve, and that longing will open the door
to their assistance; and instead of sitting in helpless despair, we shall raise our hands to them, and begin to

walk in the pathway which we shall, however, wish that we had begun to pursue while still in the earthly body.

Thank the powers that be that ordained it thus, and thank the spirits bright who have told us that it is so, we need never sit down in gloomy discouragement. Whether here or there, there is no impassable gulf between us and the brightness beyond. We may walk, we may rise, we may climb, we may fly, and rejoice forever in the boon of endless existence.

Yours for humanity and for spirituality.

LETTER FORTY-THREE.

Sadness Driven Away by a Thought Journey.

October 29, 1898.

To the Editor of THE BANNER OF LIGHT :

How beautiful the thought that whatever may be the anxieties and the perplexities of our earthly life, we can by resolute effort enter into the closet of our inner soul, shut to the door against carking care, and, by communion with the God within, reach communion with god-like souls whose companionship we crave. Such has been my experience of late, and at the present hour.

Besides carking care, which falls on me as it does on so many others in our dear country, other troubles, arising from my espousal of Spiritualism, are also to the front. For the outside world I care not; but when the opposition of those to whom I was once dear, and who continue to be very dear to me, becomes more apparent than usual, it always cuts deeply. One would fancy that my course of life since espousing this glorious Cause would begin to mitigate this contempt of me, but no : nothing can mitigate this bitter, bitter prejudice against one who does not adhere to the old orthodoxy, nor the scornful criticism, because I claim to know that the so-called dead are my helpers, my supporters, and my instructors.

So when to-day came, knowing that if I did not write to-day there would be a break in the letters that I have so assiduously provided for the BANNER OF LIGHT for nearly a year, and finding myself physically exhausted and mentally wearied, with no subject in my mind and no thought in my brain. I made my preparations, sat down to write, and have written a little bit out of my own heart.

As always, in times of stress like this, I gratefully and confidingly put my physical and spiritual body in vibration with the magnetic currents of the solar system, and my soul in harmony with pure spirits in the name of our common Source. At once came those magnetic thrills and the inner consciousness of immortal presences, and my drooping spirit was revived, like the thirsty florets who have almost gasped for life through a torrid day, but are revived by the cooling shower of evening.

I said I gratefully went through my harmonizing process, for my gratitude is continuous and expansive for being led into this safe and profitable path so soon after accepting Spiritualism. As to confiding in it, I may well do so, for never yet has it failed to put me into *rapport* with the angel-world when taken with attention.

We may know that these same magnetic currents pervade the whole solar system for this reason. As we have stated elsewhere, electricity is a force, while magnetism is a condition. A non-magnetic bar of iron becomes magnetized by being placed within a coil of wires, through which an electric current is passing. In the same way, the earth is always a magnet, owing to the currents of electricity that pass around it from its being turned upon its axis.

As the earth turns on its axis in the same way that it turns around the sun, as the moon turns on its axis and once around the earth in a lunar month in the same way, as every planet with its attendant moon and rings turns the same way, and as the sun itself revolves on its stupendous axis of eight hundred and fifty thousand miles in the same general direction, we see that the electric currents of every member of the mighty whole are similar, and the resulting magnetized conditions of each and every orb of our system are all in pure harmony.

Of course there is variety in this harmony. Our ecliptic inclines to our equinoctial enough to make a variety in our seasons that is unknown in Jupiter. But this variation must be within certain limits, and those comets that violate the general law of the system plunge off into space and are never heard of again.

It pleases me to put my outer and my inner body in harmony with these mighty currents, and my soul in harmony with the Soul of the infinite universe, then to lie down on my bed with my head toward the north, or negative, pole of the magnet, and to lie there and think far into space. My thought takes in "the earth's green pomp spinning round" (an imperfect rendition of Goethe's superbly simple line:

"Dreht sich umher der Erde Pracht").

Then I think on into the successive stages of our own spirit-world, expanding into inconceivable ethereality, and yet obedient with its earth nucleus to the electric, vortical sweep and the resulting magnetized condition. Then I think on into that still finer ether that occupies the space between the spirit-worlds of the different planets. I do not think toward the sun, the physical storehouse of electrical energy. But I think on to Mars, do not stop at the asteroids (melancholy witnesses, perhaps, of the triumph of democracy over aristocracy in the formation of the planet between Mars and Jupiter); then I think of the majestic Jupiter and the ringed Saturn and quiet Uranus, and lonely Neptune, 2,800,-000,000 miles from the sun. Then I think of still more distant comets, and am amazed at the mighty force which holds many of them to their periodical journeys around the sun. The address of the "Ettrick Shepherd" to the comet of 1811 comes to my mind, and I recall one of the stanzas:

> "On thy rapid prow to glide,
>   To sail the boundless skies with thee,
> And plough the twinkling stars aside,
>   Like foam-bells on a tranquil sea!"

and wish that I could recall the rest.

Then, as thought has no seeming limit, I think on of other systems of worlds, of double suns of complementary tints revolving around each other, each with its own retinue of planets, and am dazed at the mathematics involved in keeping them all aright, far transcending the geometrical problems involved in our own system with its single sun.

I think, too, of our sun as being a subordinate member of that nebula we call the Milky Way, as is proved by our seeing it as a ring around us, instead of viewing it as a whole, as we view the nebula in Andromeda.

Then I think of Thoreau and his bright and characteristic reply to some one who said to him: "Mr. Thoreau, I should think you would be lonely, living out here in the woods by yourself." "Lonely," said he, "how can I feel lonely? Is not our sun in the Milky Way?"

So I come back to earth and Walden Pond and the sages of Concord and the peerless Emerson, fittingly called St. Ralph. Murmuring "God bless him, wherever he may be," I fall asleep.

Yours for humanity and for spirituality.

LETTER FORTY-FOUR.

Opinions regarding Jesus.

November 3, 1898.

To the Editor of THE BANNER OF LIGHT:

Some twenty-five years ago I heard James Freeman Clarke illustrate the presentation of Jesus of Nazareth by the four Evangelists in the following manner. He said it was like putting Jesus in the centre of four mirrors that were placed around him. The reflection in each mirror was a different one, and yet the union of the four showed him as he was.

As an illustration, it was good, and, had all four been written by eye-witnesses while their subject still walked the earth, the picture might have been as true as other pictures of famous men. But when we recollect that the two written soon after his resurrection give a simple narration of facts; that the third, written perhaps thirty years later, brings out his sacrificial nature, which doctrine had meantime become a part of Christianity; and that the fourth, written generations after the others, presents the dogma of incarnate deity, which had in the meantime been incorporated by many into the body of doctrine, we see that Mr. Clarke's illustration was not founded on the facts of the case.

Still, this illustration of Jesus and the four mirrors is applicable to many a subject which occupies the human mind, and we are sometimes led with Pilate of old to ask. "What is truth?"

No character has been more discussed than that of Christ. Those about him said, "Never man spake like this man," recognizing him as a man among men. Later, that he was an incarnate God came to be surmised, and this doctrine was adopted as an article of church doctrine by the first Nicean Council in 325, A.D. This was emphasized at the Council of Chalcedon in 451, which also proclaimed Mary to be "the mother of

God," in opposition to Nestorius, who claimed her to be only the mother of his human nature. The same was reiterated at Constantinople in 553.

From this time the diety of Jesus has held sway in the Christian Church, and was disputed only by those who denied the Bible to be the word of God, like Voltaire and Frederic the Great.

In our century, in which human reason, blunted and stunted in previous ages, has burst into bloom and the "higher criticism" has waxed stronger and stronger, the metaphysical doubts of German thinkers, the aggressive efforts of French skeptics, and the publication of such works as Strauss's and Renan's lives of Jesus, have reduced the doctrine of an incarnate deity to a dogma, held to only by the most conservative adherents to the old Orthodoxy.

Meanwhile Spiritualism has been throwing a new light into many an obscure and tangled nook in the records of the past. It has shown that some of the most extraordinary events recorded in the Hebrew Bible are duplicated by mediums of modern times, and are thus divested of all supernatural quality. It has shown that Socrates derived his power from his consciousness of a guiding spirit, whose voice he heard. It has shown that Joan of Arc was a clairvoyant and a clairaudient medium, and accomplished the liberation of France through the assistance of decarnate and patriotic Frenchmen. It has shown that Mohammed was a trance medium, instead of an epileptic impostor. It has shown that the world's greatest poets, orators, artists, and inventors were susceptible to spirit influence, and that genius is itself an extraordinary phase of mediumship, working on a highly endowed brain.

We expect Buddhists and Taoists to take but scant interest in the assumption that Jesus of Nazareth was an incarnated God. But the question is of considerable interest to those who live within the pale of Christendom, and especially those of us who were brought up to worship him, and to pray to him, exactly as if he were indeed and in truth "very God of very God.'

And our church friends, too, desire to know what we think that our spirit-friends have to say of Jesus.

One would naturally suppose that we who claim to be in intelligent communication with the spirit-world could now get something definite, harmonious and integral regarding Jesus. Did he ever live at all? Was he Appollonius of Tyana? Was there anything extraordinary about his birth? Was he an incarnation of "God over all blessed forever"? Was he the God of this planet? Have any spirits ever met him, and talked with him? Does he ever control mediums? What does he say about the four gospels? Had he in any sense more of the divine nature than inheres in all human beings? Was he just a great healing medium?

To any and all of these questions we receive through various mediums the most contradictory answers. In fact, there seems to be nearly as many answers as mediums. Robert Dale Owen's lovely spirit friend, "Violet" says that Jesus was born from a perfectly pure Jewish virgin. The medium through whom "Antiquity Unveiled" was given to mortals, under the supervision of the learned and sincere J. M. Roberts, says no such man as Jesus ever lived, and has communications from scores of spirits never heard of in America, though said to be in obscure and ancient European encyclopædias. Dr. J. R. Buchanan on the other hand says he has talked with Jesus and the apostels, and that they are *bona fide* individuals.

A very lovely medium in Providence, R. I., now in spirit, claimed that she was the scribe of Jesus, Mary, Joseph, and many other friends of the Nazarene. She saw the words printed in electric light, and wrote exactly what she saw. In her book, "The Autobiography of Jesus of Nazareth," he claims to be a mere man, a meek, ailing, hunch-backed man, but strong when controlled by Leiah, once King of Arabia, whom he calls his father, though Joseph and Mary were his real father and mother.

Some mediums teach that one special spirit, god of this planet, is incarnated once in about six hundre years. He was Confucius, he was Jesus, he was Mohammed, seems not to have manifested in the thirteenth century (unless Dante were he), but will now soon appear.

In all these conflicting accounts what are we to believe? I say, nothing at all, and for two reasons. One reason is, that what comes through mediums, or to us personally as individual spirits, is so tinctured by their or our previous opinions and prejudices, hereditary biases and spiritual affinities, that it is not very reliable regarding personalities and facts that have to do with past existence on the earth planet.

The other reason is, that it is not what we *believe* that matters, it what we *do*. It matters little to us whether Jesus existed personally or not, provided we live as purely and as lovingly as he is said to have done. It matters not whether he was immaculately conceived; but it matters whether we live immaculately ourselves. Are we to-day humane, kind, truthful, brave, industrious and reverent? If so, we are preparing to be more so to morrow,

> "And better thence again, and better still,
>   In infinite progression."

Yours for humanity and for spirituality.

LETTER FORTY-FIVE.

A Tolerant Spirit.

November 10, 1898.

To the Editor of THE BANNER OF LIGHT:

Before taking up the subject of this letter, I will speak of a personal matter that will be omitted if deferred. As I say nothing of my sight, and keep up these weekly letters for THE BANNER, and as we naturally hope for the well being of our friends, it is supposed that my eyes are all right and give me no more trouble. Alas! it is not so.

My right eye, operated on in New York, is all right; but the left eye becomes worse, and gives me constant pain when I use the good one for reading, writing, or sewing. I have had lens after lens made for it. Each does well for a time, but in a few weeks the ball of the eye has altered again and I cannot see. I cannot always have new lenses made, and now I cannot see one word with this eye; and its constant effort to see, when I use the other, is what gives the pain; and an oculist will understand why, when I add that its iris is incarcerated. The constant change in form is the result of the escape of so much of the vitreous, when the wound broke open after the operation in Worcester. Neither of these conditions can be removed by art.

It seemed strange to many that Gladstone, so devoted to the interests of the Church of England, to which he belonged, should hold those religious views that belong to the Unitarians and the Semites, and that he was in heart a deist rather than a Christian. It seems stranger on this side of the water, where we are indoctrinated with the thought of a complete separation between the church and the government. But not so with our British cousins. The union between the church and the State over there makes many a man conventionally accord with the church, while his real opinions are quite variant therefrom. Ever since Henry the Eighth put himself at the head of the church instead of the Pope, so far as England was concerned, each reigning king and queen occupies that position, and of course subscribes wholly to all its tenets in public life.

Long ago, when I believed in the inspiration by God of the whole Bible, which states quite clearly immersion and believers' baptism, I was simple enough to wonder what a king of England could do if he should become a convert to the views of Calvinistic Baptists. If he should be immersed and believe in close communion, what would become of his headship over the Church of England? But, in later years, it became easy to see that this perfunctory head could in heart adopt any religious faith in the world, yea, be even an atheist, and yet serenely pose, by virtue of his sovereignty, as the head of the Established Church of England. On this same principle, Gladstone could partake of the eucharist and yet adopt the views of an orthodox Jew.

And among all the sects in Christendom there is hardly one so tolerant of the religious views of others as are the Jews. It has not been their habit to proselyte, even from the early individualization of the race. Ancient Israel believed in the God of the Jews, and contentedly let their neighbors go on worshiping their own gods. While they thought it idolatry if one of their own race adored a foreign idol, they were willing that other races should worship Baal and Osiris, Astarte and Chemosh, at their pleasure. This Jewish principle is expressed by both instance and precept in the Old Testament.

The other day, while looking up some passages in the sacred writings of the Jews, I came across this in Micah. This forcible and earnest seer is describing the future glory when war will be unknown, and each man shall sit in safety under his own fig tree. Recognizing that intolerance has caused much bloodshed, he goes on to say: " *For* all people will walk everyone in the name of *his* god, and *we* will walk in the name of the Lord *our* God."

I was greatly struck by the open religious toleration so plainly inculcated by this ancient Jew; and noted well that the Christian church, while advocating the peace spoken of in the third verse, yet utterly ignores the tolerant views given in the context, and goes to work to induce other nations to discard their own deities and to adopt that form of idolatry so prevalent in the Christian church of to-day.

Lessing's drama, " Nathan the Wise," has three principal characters: Nathan, a Jew; Saladin, a Mohammedan; and the Templar, a Christian. In the play occurs the apt and beautiful story of the ring, of which I will give a synopsis.

A king possessed a priceless ring, which made its owner beloved by God and man. Having three sons equally dear to him, and not knowing what else to do, he had two more rings made exactly like the first, gave one to each son, and died. Disputes arose as to which had the true ring. These continued till a wise judge arose, who said: "Let each one of you deem his own true, and *make* it true by displaying the most gentleness, forbearance, charity, and heartfelt resignation to God's will. If after thousands of years these virtues appear in your posterity, perhaps a wiser judge than I can decide which had the true ring."

By this tale did Nathan, the wise Jew, teach Saladin and the Templar to try to settle by the result on their posterity which of the three religions was the true one. The story, borrowed from the storehouse of Boccaccio, illustrates Lessing's views of religious tolerance, and suggests the only practical solution. No religion is the exclusive religion of the world. All have their uses, in different ages and with different races; and as mankind spiritualizes in its progress godward, the simplest religion—love to God and love to man, divested of every shred of form, and having its seat within each human soul—will prevail.

May a progressive Spiritualist counts himself a Christian? Most certainly, if we understand the word Christian aright. If being a Christian involve a belief in being saved by the blood shed on Calvary, and in the deity of the man Jesus, I am not a Christian. But if it mean a constant determination to imitate the pure and the benevolent Nazarene in his virtues, then I *am* a Christian, and no bigot shall take from me this name. Yea, verily, in the true sense of this word, I have a right to this name, though I prefer the far wider and deeper name of Spiritualist. Christian is a word derived from the name of a man, a Jew; Spiritualist is as broad as Infinite Spirit, which is Infinite Soul, expressed by an Infinite Universe.

Yours for humanity and for spirituality.

LETTER FORTY-SIX.

Self-Development Without Mortal Aid.

November 17, 1898.

To the Editor of THE BANNER OF LIGHT:

Many letters that I receive are truly pathetic. Some are from persons whose strange experiences with professional mediums have almost driven them out of Spiritualism, but who turn to me as their anchor because I am so sure that its claims are true. Some write that just as they are developing into mediumship they are beset by undeveloped spirits, who desire to take control of them. Still another class think that if they could have a personal talk with me, or have me come and visit them at their own home, I could do such work with them that they would doubt no more.

To all these persons I would say that there is enough strength, wisdom, and purity in the spiritual realms to supply *all* their needs, and that what they have to do is to put themselves in harmony with it. Instead of thinking that if they could only see this one or that one they would be all right, thus leaning upon "an arm of flesh," they need to begin in solitude with their own individual self.

Let them strictly ascertain what is the governing purpose of the life they lead (for we all have one main governing purpose in life, though we lose sight of it sometimes through passion, or a desire to please some one), and carefully note the motives that underlie their acts. The importance of this inquiry lies in the fact that upon our governing purpose, or our motives, depends the nature of the spirits who find an open doorway into the inner sanctum of our being.

For instance, if our main object is to get money, if on meeting persons or going to places our hidden inquiry is, "How can I make this serve the condition of my pecuniary gains?" we open the door to mercenary spirits. If we often feel unkindly or suspiciously to those with whom we live, then some murderer or other vicious spirit builds a nest within the citadel of our being, from which it will be difficult to dislodge him. If, all unknown to mortals, we indulge in unclean thoughts and imaginings, this fact is perfectly patent to lascivious spirits, who are attracted by the same; and they delightedly flock in, fan the impure flame, and indulge their repressed longing for sensual gratification at the expense of our own organism. As we thus open the door to unprogressive and earth bound spirits, the higher ones are excluded, and turn sorrowfully away. So it is of paramount importance to look well within, and remember that we attract beings who are similar to ourselves, until we become, by communion with high, powerful spirits, so developed that we can be used as their instruments to aid poor souls fettered by low longings and reminiscences, from true liberty.

It is easy to fancy that being with strong people will bring us strength. But strength thus imbibed is only a seeming strength, and does not stand the test of an emergency. Just as our own muscles do not gain power by our watching the feats of a trained gymnast, so our spiritual powers do not gain by our sitting near and looking at those whose inner nature has " become strong by struggling." Some one spoke a noble truth when he said, "If we conquer a difficulty, the strength of the difficulty passes into us." The only way to become stronger is to *use* whatever strength we already have.

A little further back I spoke of examining ourselves in solitude. Some are so environed that they can very seldom be alone. In that case they may be quite sure that the steady wish of their heart meets a ready response from the spiritual realms, and that angels of sympathy and helpfulness send them threads of strength that will in time become cable cords through the co-operative efforts of the seeking mortal and the helpful spirits. So ready are they to aid that

> " The upward glancing of an eye,
> The falling of a tear "

are always noted by them, and they come on swift wings to aid us though we be unconscious of their aid.

The lesson taught to us by our ministering loved ones is this: Look not too much to other mortals, still environed like you with a fleshly body, the things of sense, and with about all they can do to keep their own little light a burning. Cast out every unkind thought, trample down every passion, think of the spiritual world of which you are really a denizen, think of the immortal power that is really yours if you will only lay hold of it, think of the golden spiritual links that bind all souls together (your soul, too, though it may be but a tiny one), think that bright angels note your aspirations, and do the bidding of those still more advanced, in short, trust the soul power of the universe in which you dwell, and drink in help from radiant ones who are strong enough to impart to you.

Having so done, turn to your daily work—to your husband, your wife, your child, your associates- and remember that every kind word you speak, every smile on your face, every room you neatly sweep, every hungry creature you feed, whether human or animal, every nail you thoroughly drive, every lesson you understandingly learn, every impatient word repressed, every frown suppressed. every cold horse whose blanket you replace, every appreciative word you speak, every dollar you give away, in short every true and kind word, thought and deed, is ennobling your manhood and your womanhood, and is thus making you a brighter and more helpful spirit when the clay shackles drop away. Then those glorious spirits whose care you are, will say, "Our little struggling child has done well, and shall now have a holiday in our beautiful world." There is a sweet day coming for you by and by, over burdened soul.

Some feel sure they would be happy if they were only millionaires What a mistake! The poor millionaires have many a care that we know nothing of ; and I am sure that I would not exchange my body, washed *a la* Dio Lewis every morning, and nourished on plain, wholesome food, for the pampered body of Mrs. Millionaire, steamed in hot baths, stuffed with every abomination of the rich man's table, stimulated by coffee and poisoned by champagne. Look at her horse, in agony with his curb-bit, his tight check-rein, and no tail to keep the flies off in summer, and no hair to keep the cold off in winter. Look at her fat poodle. He can hardly waddle, so full is he of cake and spiced meat, and never a good run without a chain. No, no; I would not exchange places with Mr. Millionaire or his wife.

By and by they will be ill. Surgeons, skilled by much vivisection of despairing dogs and pitiable rabbits, will now operate on them. But they cannot save them, and they die. They are heaped over with flowers costly enough to feed a regiment of starving soldiers, and ponderous marble monuments will celebrate the imagined virtues of those whose bodies lie below.

They will awake in spirit life. What will they have? He will look for his bankbook and his certificates of stocks, his horses and his wines, but he cannot find them. She will sit and call for her lady's maid and her diamonds, her coachman and her furs, but they will not be there. They will be dazed and desolate for a long time ; but after a while they will begin to earn the things that are of real value, for there is hope in a universe where the law of love is the final appeal, for even a monopolist and a millionaire.

Yours for humanity and for spirituality.

LETTER FORTY-SEVEN.

Real Evidence.

November 26, 1898.

To the Editor of THE BANNER OF LIGHT :

The rich verdue of the morning-glories has black-ened, and the twisted stems look bare in this Thanks-giving snow.   But under the snow, the drifting leaves, and the gathering soil many seeds lie hidden, and will gladden us with abundant bloom when our planet reaches another quarter of the ecliptic.   And with the precious self-sown seed of my own plants, I expect to delightedly watch those that will grow from the seeds sent me by that dear friend of the Cause, Mrs. Anna K. Clifford of Cleveland.   Hers will be lovely indeed, " of unusual size, a beautiful blue in color, with a horizontal rim of white at the outer edge, while the neck of the flower shows a rosy tinge."

I have just formed the acquaintance of "The Lyceum," published by her husband, Mr. Tom Clifford, and illumined by her gentle spirit.   I am very much taken by this weekly, and recommend it to all Spiritualists who desire their own children and those of others to be both entertained and enlightened by this admirable little paper.

Several years ago I cut out from the *Religio-Philo-sophical Journal* a short article by Minot J. Savage, en-titled "Evidence."   It gave me much to think of at the time, and was the key-note to much that has come to me since, regarding spiritual phenomena.   I have just re-read it, and it seems to me just as valuable as when it first met my eyes.

His first point is that no iteration of the statement, " I know it is so," is sufficient ; the facts must be es-tablished by evidence that would satisfy a court of justice.   His second point is, that we must not call in the spirits of the dead as an explanation, till every other conceivable theory has been shown to be inadequate. The spirit theory must be proved as clearly as is the fact that the earth is a sphere.

He recommends that those who have had a remarkable experience write it out as accurately as possible, and settle the date, if that can be done, and have others who were present do the same.. Also, if you have in the future such an experience, record it at once, whether you know that it comes true or not. Then tell some one of it at once, and get this person to witness your record. Third, if it comes out true, make a written record of this new fact, and have as many persons witness this record as possible. Always set down the dates.

This is the true way to get an accumulation of real evidence. By so doing we can put it out of the power of opponents to say, "You *think* you saw such and such a thing," "You imagined that," or, "You and the persons with you were psychologized." That last objection is painfully amusing, as it is spiritual investigation alone that has taught christendom the possibility of being psychologized.

It is the pursuance of such methods that caused that immense audience at the closing session of the World's Psychical Congress in Chicago in 1893 to hang with breathless attention on the words of F. W. H. Myers of England. And it is his rigid adherence to such methods that has given so rare a value to the investigations of Dr. Hodgson, and to his frank and fearless statement of the conclusion he has reached.

Not long ago a gentleman residing in the Middle West sent me a photograph of a life size portrait of his relative, believed to be taken through the psychic power of a well-known medium in Chicago. On the back of the photograph is a printed account of the way this portrait was produced, and it makes the claim that this special phenomenon gave absolute *evidence* of the truth of spirit-existence and spirit-return.

And yet a careful examination of this printed statement reveals so many flaws that its value as direct evidence is reduced to *nil.* It is precisely one of those narrations that are convincing to Spiritualists, but do not convince non-Spiritualists who are accustomed to weighing evidence.

To premise, the originalof the portrait, a well-known resident of the town where this gentleman resides, passed to spirit-life in 1888. In 1891 the gentleman began his investigations into Spiritualism with the same medium and her companion through whom this portrait was obtained, in 1897, and was convinced through them that Spiritualism is true. I was in that town in 1891, conversed with this gentleman, and remember the facts of the case. During the intervening six years he continued his acquaintance with these two mediums, and they had ample opportunity to search out all facts connected with his dead relatives.

When this "convincing" manifestation took place in 1897, he was at the residence of the mediums, in a room alone with one of them. He had brought the canvas for the portrait with him. He placed the canvas under a table in the middle of the room, a curtain was pinned around the table, and he and the medium waited, while engaged in conversation. He expressly states that the medium had never seen his dead relative, nor a picture of him. He does not give any proof of this. Could he have been with that medium every day and night during those six years, and known in that way that she had never seen his picture? Or, did he make this statement on the word of the medium herself?

At the end of three hours he heard three taps upon the table, then, "no one else having touched the canvas after he had placed it there," he took it out and found a life-size portrait of his dead relative.

He does not state that he had made a thorough examination of the floor, nor of the ceiling of the room directly below it. We do not therefore see a solid ground for his statement that no one had touched the canvas after he had placed it there. Remember that the occurrence took place at the residence of the two mediums. How can he *prove* that during the three hours his canvas was not taken through the floor, and the portrait prepared beforehand, and now marked to duplicate his own canvas, not substituted? Three hours gave ample time for all this to be done.

We hope not to be misunderstood. We know more remarkable things than this have been done by decarnate spirits under proved conditions that made explanation impossible only on the spirit hypothesis. What we mean to say is that the account of this manifestation and a majority of ordinary manifestations, leaves too many exposed places and too many flaws to allow it to be taken as actual evidence of the intervention of decarnate spirits.

I have myself been perfectly cognizant of many instances of spiritual manifestation that could be accounted for only on the spiritual hypothesis. I have also been personally cognizant of many manifestations that could have been accounted for by the intervention of mortals alone, but which I believe to have been genuine, from the nature of the medium, from the internal evidence of the communication, and from the likelihood that the spirits would avail themselves of the opportunity. And I have been personally cognizant of a very few instances where fraud was intentionally used by a bogus medium.

It is for the skeptical outside world that we insist that evidence be irrefragable, that there be no loop-hole where the enemy's arrow can find entrance. But when we commune with our dear decarnate friends, we demand nothing of the sort. Then it is "Soul to soul, like the blending of light do our souls mingle." And the same lofty spirit wrote me on one occasion, "The soul needs no tongue, my child." But these communings are naught to the "madding crowd," though they are everything to the happy recipient. On such occasions we do not think of a test. Indeed, the very word is repugnant. But when we seek to bring a manifestation to the notice of the outside world, in order to convince them that Spiritualism is true, we demand the clearest, the strongest and the most impregnable *evidence.*

Yours for humanity and for spirituality.

N. B.—It is proper to state that the gentleman who received the portrait as described, states later that he had previously marked the canvas he brought with him in such a way that it could not be duplicated ; that the portrait differs from any likeness that was ever taken of his dead relative ; that he selected the place in the room where the table should be placed, and made a thorough examination of the carpet ; and that though he did not examine the ceiling of the room below, that very room was occupied by persons who were waiting for a sitting, while this portrait was being produced. The only mistake was in omitting those circumstances in the original account.

LETTER FORTY-EIGHT.

Old Age Transfigured by Spiritualism.

December 2, 1898.

To the Editor of THE BANNER OF LIGHT :

Why is it that when sweetness and light have come into the world, the great bulk of mankind, even in what are called the enlightened nations of the earth, are nearly unconscious of them ?

I was led to this inquiry by the opening of an able article by Mr. Griffis in *The Outlook* of Nov. 26, entitled " America in the Far East." He says in youth we listen to the voice of hope; in maturity, to that of cheer; in old age, to that of warning. He asks whether we as a nation are at man's estate or in old age: if the former, we listen to the voice of cheer; if the latter, to that of discouragement.

This writer does not stand alone in this view of old age. He has precisely the general view of mankind; and there is not a religion in the world that has succeeded in making its votaries look at old age in any other way than this. Neither has there been a philosophy in the world that has gone any further than to make it wisdom in old age to be resigned to it, and to surrender unmurmuring to what is inevitable.

As I took in the sense of Mr. Griffis' illustration, my whole soul rose within me to think that the world in general are so blind to the natural facts revealed by Spiritualism *alone* as to think that old age is in any sense a period of gloom and discouragement. And so accustomed are they to this view that it does not occur to them that there is any other way to do. From the time of Solomon, who pictures so vividly the time when the grasshopper shall be a burden and desire shall fail, to our own generation here in America who dread the thought of growing old, the longing of mortals has been to drink of the fountain of perpetual youth. Even do the Christian Scientists sympathize with this fear of old age by promising that if one only follow their maxims, he need never grow old, he need never die.

Perhaps the main point of the dread of old age lies in the proverb, "The young may die, but the old must." As long as death is feared and dreaded, so long will all the avenues that lead to it, as illness and old age, be also feared. Ah! me, how well I remember the fainting of heart, the desperate shrinking with which I noted the passage of decade after decade of my mortal career, and saw the narrowing and darkening vista, to be closed in at last by the tomb!

And what I felt is felt by millions, and the only panacea is forgetting it, or taking refuge in the blood of Jesus. Ah! the pity of it, and the needlessness of it!

Some of my readers will remember Dame Quickly's account of the death of Falstaff. He cried out several times, "God, God, God." To comfort him she bade him not to think of God; that she hoped there was no need to trouble himself with any such thoughts yet. But thoughts of God and old age and death itself had to come upon poor old Jack, and even on the master magician who created him, and who knew much, but did not know what you and I know, dear reader, that death is not death at all, but a mere gateway between a lower life and a higher life.

There is no good in thinking that the closing years of life are all right if we are washed in Calvary's blood, and that death is sweet if we are only in the arms of Jesus, for these are mere fancies, and have no solid ground of truth. And the thought that taking up such fancies is going to do away with the effect of a misspent life is wrong as well as foolish.

A friend of my youth published in 1872 a very interesting Christian story. The heroine is at one time tending the deathbed of her father, who had lived a wholly useless and selfish life. This conversation is recorded:

"Margaret, what shall I do?"

"Nothing, dear father, Jesus has done everything."

"Will his sacrifice cover the guilt of a wasted life?"

"Dear father, yes. It covers everything. The blood of Jesus Christ cleanseth us from all sin."

So did the man in the story, and many a man in actual life, pass into the life beyond hugging to himself the false notion that another's good deeds can be placed to our account, and give them the standing that can be acquired only by one's own acts.

The old-time friend who wrote that story married an Englishman, and has lived in England many years. I spent a month with them in their beautiful home early in 1877. Fresh from Paris and from the ministrations of the eloquent M. Bersier, I used to repeat French hymns to her, and try to fortify her faltering soul by trusting in Jesus; for she could not then rely implicitly on the teachings of her own book. Some dozen years later I joyfully wrote her of the new, exquisite light that was brightening so gloriously the narrowing vista of my mortal life. I wrote again and again, and a few years ago her brother-in-law, a minister in this country, wrote me the following words when I wrote to him after my brother's transition, and my heart turned yet again to those who had tenderly loved him in the far-away days of youth: "Mrs. ——'s very radical antago-

nism to the spiritualistic views you have adopted may
have led her to feel that it was best to discontinue an
intercourse which could no longer be maintained on the
old footing. This is a better way than to combat what
one disapproves, or to seem to countenance it by passing
it over in silence." So I remain silent because I must,
and wait for the light that will surely come " when the
mists have cleared away."

Having now given some thought to the view that
makes old age either a period of gloom and discouragement, or else cheered by hopes that are wholly fantas-
tic and illusory, let us see what old age is to those who
are now experiencing it in the dawn of the light of
Spiritualism.

Spiritualism, or rather Naturalism, as I am more and
more inclined to call it, shows us that death is not a
finality, but an onward step in the progress of individual life. This being so, old age, which naturally leads
up to this graduating day, becomes to those who have
lived a well spent life, a period of great encouragement,
cheer, and abounding hopes. This were true, even
though one were to be solitary, both here and there.
But when to this is added our knowledge of the fact
that all whom we have dearly loved or deeply revered,
who disappeared from mortal sight in our childhood, our
youth, in the different stages of our maturity, and in
advancing years, are more joyfully alive than before,
still note our career with interest and love, and are
awaiting the time when they can lead us into the joys
of the spirit-land, old age becomes a time of more than
cheer and encouragement. It becomes a time of joyful hope, and of well-nigh realization of what is so
imminent.

> "My angels come and walk with me,
> And sweet communion here have we;
> They gently lead me by the hand,
> For this is heaven's borderland."

These are some of the more obvious reasons why old
age is a time of joy to those who are so happy as to see
the sweetness and the light that have come into the

world. When to this is added the growing consciousness of an imminent and beneficent indwelling soul in
all things, of which we are part and parcel; that our
upward strivings are helping to spiritualize the universe
itself; that the process here begun is destined to bear
bloom and fruitage on life's fair tree beyond our present power to conceive; and that we shall see the
increasing bliss of those whom we have loved, and
whose woes have given us anguish while here below,
we feel the dawnings of an estatic joy that mortal
tongue cannot express. Youth is sweet and full of
hope, maturity brings the joy of work, of duty patiently
fulfilled, but old age brings with it the happiness that
springs from the angelic assurance that heaven is near,
that our loved ones are waiting and watching, and that
we shall soon, yea, very soon, be with them in their
ineffable and tranquil joy.

Yours for humanity and for spirituality.

LETTER FORTY-NINE.

Revering Those Beyond and Above us.

December 8, 1898.

To the Editor of THE BANNER OF LIGHT:

In my last letter I spoke of the great delight felt in
old age by those who are walking the latter part of
life's pilgrimage in the cheering light of Spiritualism,
and of the impotence of the different religions and of
philosophy itself to bring the same illumination.

As has been stated before, only those dwell in
heaven, whether embodied or disembodied, who love
and aid all beings inferior to them in any respect, who
love with just dealing those on a par with themselves,
and who love and revere all beings who are superior to
themselves in those qualities that denote the true progress of the soul. We claim that this mental attitude
alone betokens a real spiritual progress. If we do not

love and compassionate our inferiors, we have a tendency to tyranny, and need to beware. If we do not love and deal justly with our equals, we cannot be in the heavenly state, and if we do not love and revere those who have attained the higher rounds of the spiritual ladder, it looks as if we esteem ourselves so much that we cannot acknowledge the superiority of another, besides losing the powerful stimulus which is begotten by the desire to attain what they have attained.

Alas! in this world there are many who act as if their possessing the power gave them the right to maim and torture the lower animals, to rob the defenseless of their money and their property, to beat a child, to abuse a woman, and to stab a sensitive heart with cruel words and slanderous suspicions. It is the mission of Spiritualism to teach its votaries to do exactly opposite to this ; and by thus placing an object lesson before those who know us most intimately, cause a true humanity to go like leaven from heart to heart until this earth has become indeed the wished-for heaven

As to loving and treating with absolute fairness those who are on our level, it can only be practised by those in whom selfishness has been stamped out. The selfish person sees his own needs, he is blind to those of his neighbor. His wanting a thing is reason enough for him to seize it. If he is in low life he may be a pickpocket. If he belongs to the upper ten, he may be a great monopolist. If he likes to talk, he monopolizes all the conversation. If the person be an attractive young man or woman, he tries to make as many of the opposite sex enamored with him as possible. If he is a doctor, a lawyer, or a minister, he feels angry at those who may surpass him in paying patients, in easily gulled clients, and in the number of devoted and wealthy parishioners, and will by sly innuendoes and tricky ways, try to divert all valuable patronage to himself. True love, the love " which seeketh not her own," is the only panacea for such moral corruption as this.

A gentle, tender, and helpful spirit toward the weak lays the foundation of an angelic character; equal and absolute justice toward our equals bespeaks the rounding out of a manly development; but it is to our third point, a reverence toward those whose present status is the goal we seek, that we now ask the attention of those who would tread supernal paths.

To be able to revere is a lofty gift of the soul. Its expression is wanting in many, though the germ, like every other spiritual seed, is innately implanted and will in time develop. We are grieved when we hear a person say that he reverences no one. It is usually a young person who says this, and such a one tells the truth, and it makes one pity him. Persons more advanced in life have learned to revere those who possess virtues greater than their own. Though they may themselves be what the world calls bad, they feel that reverence is due, though they do not try to imitate. But young persons of the type adverted to do not know enough to revere. They will learn some time in the future, and the new consciousness will flood their souls with a sweetness at present all unknown.

Such a one sometimes excuses his want of reverence, or veneration, by declaring that those feelings should be felt toward God alone. But to be able to revere the absolute, the illimitable, the unconditioned, one must begin by feeling thus toward the lesser beings that one can take within one's own comprehension. As one of old asked how one could love God, whom he had not seen, unless he love his brother, whom he had seen, so do we question how one can revere the Infinite without revering the beings whom we know who merit it? In other words, a feeling due to unconditioned being is the expansion of the germ that begins to work on the objects and the persons near at hand.

I am glad to be able to reverence finite beings who are worthy of being reverenced; and I would far rather revere Ralph Waldo Emerson, who was possessed of purity, nobility, and an almost matchless humility, than such a God as Moses taught the Jews to worship. That

God was revengeful, selfish, cruel, and extremely jealous. He himself declared that he was so jealous that it made him angry if a Jew worshipped any other god. As to the Ten Commandments, it is not to the credit of the Jewish race at that ancient time to have to be told not to do such things as are alluded to in most of the ten.

Doubtless some of your readers have heard what a Japanese said about these ten Mosaic injunctions. Some zealot had brought them to his notice. After reading them, the Japanese quietly remarked: "They are well written and well put together; but my people do not need to be told not to do such things, as they do not do them."

In my vain efforts to find some denomination of Christianity with which I could affiliate, I at one time went a good deal to the Episcopal church. Though I tried to give it a fair trial and be very devout, it did seem queer to me to respond: "Lord, have mercy on me, and incline my heart to keep this law," after hearing the clergyman read, "Thou shalt not kill, thou shalt not commit adultery, thou shalt not steal," and the rest of it. I do not remember ever wanting to do any of these things.

Dharmapala said a grand thing, though it would be scouted by those who advocate the "righteousness being filthy rags" theory. This wise Hindoo said that the greatest happiness conceivable is to be conscious of one's own purity. May all we love and all who love us have much of this kind of happiness! Then shall we be more and more revered as old age advances, and when liberation day comes, we shall joyfully ascend to dwell with those whom we have revered on high.

Yours for humanity and for spirituality.

LETTER FIFTY.

Intensely Cold Weather and Its Cause.

December 15, 1898.

To the Editor of THE BANNER OF LIGHT:

There is a very good man near here who will go straight to heaven when he "dies." I do not know what denomination of Christianity claims him for her own. He may be a Roman Catholic for aught I know. He may be a Methodist. The only indicator of his religious proclivities is that his son is named Calvin, and yet that indicates nothing, as that too suggestive name may be a family heirloom with the ancestral Calvinism worn threadbare. But this man is surely going to heaven when he dies, and we will now tell the reason why. Last Tuesday night, the coldest of the season so far, this man took in five outcast dogs and let them lie in his kitchen all night. They lay in comfort, while the bitter wind raged without, and I in my warm bed could not sleep for thinking of the homeless and hungry dogs and cats, the poorly sheltered horses and cows, the aged shivering under insufficient clothing, with scanty fuel, and the little children of the drunkard who have no warm bedding, no thick socks and shoes, no warm, nourishing food, because the money of the author of their being has been squandered for the most baleful thing that has cursed humanity, the alcoholic stimulant.

Such nights I cannot sleep, for thinking that if it be so cold in New Jersey, what must it be in the unprotected stretches of Minnesota and the adjacent regions. On these prairies there is no wood, and the unsheltered brutes—unable to find turf beneath the snow, nor a drop of water, for it is frozen solid—fall before the merciless blizzard and perish by the thousand. Little, little does the minion of fortune know of the pain, the agony endured by man and beast in inclement, wintry weather.

I heard of a rich woman who went out for a short drive on a bitter cold winter day. Her finely caparisoned horses needed the exercise, and she went to buy some furbelow at fashion's bazaar. Noting the extreme cold, which penetrated even her sealskin wrappings, she thought of a poor woman she knew who probably had no fuel. She bade her coachman telephone to her coal-dealer to send a quarter of a ton of coal to this woman's home, and sank back amid her luxurious cushions in the serene consciousness that she had done a remarkably good deed.

But alas! On reaching her exquisitely appointed home, after the maid had removed her wraps, and she felt the summer heat of the whole mansion, she concluded that it was not very cold after all, and that she had made a mistake. So she bade her coachman countermand the order, and no coal was sent to the poor woman.

To return to this very good man who took in the five freezing dogs, I must add that his wife will also go to heaven when she dies; for she not only made no opposition to receiving her four-footed guests, but gave them a warm reception, and did not let them go supperless to bed.

Before quitting this subject, I must say a word of little Calvin. He is said to be a naughty boy. In spite of this, or it may be because of this, he is a great favorite with me. If he comes to my house after he has gone I hasten to see what he has unscrewed, or unwound, or undone. And as he knows that piercing and dismal shrieks will surely bring him the thing he craves, he startles all within hearing by his determined outcries, while those who know say it is only Calvin who wants something. Of course he is too much of a philosopher to cry for what there is no hope of obtaining. He believes in the "conservation of energy."

I always liked the boy, but especially since the following incident. One day on a walk the conversation turned on Calvin's naughtiness On the principle that

it makes children bad to treat them as if they are bad,
I said, "Oh! no; he is a *good* boy. I know he will be
a good boy." His aunt chimed in with me and said,
"Yes, he is going to be a very good boy." Startled by
this prospect that seemed to be opening before him, all
the elf could say was, "When?" His dark, gloomy
eyes showed his recoil from entering such new paths.
I have seldom been more amused, and hope it will be
many a day before little Calvin will walk demurely
therein.

Ever since living for thirteen years in Minneapolis,
noting the bitter complaints of human beings regarding
the intensity of the cold, and the dumb anguish of the
helpless brutes, I have pondered on the original cause
of what is so obviously wrong. In the old days it was
thought to be very wicked to find fault with rain or
snow, or heat or cold, because all these things were
manifestations of the personal will of a personal God, and
to rebel against the weather was to rebel against him,
and might, if persisted in, cause the rebel to be struck
dead.

Of course it all looks very different now. I have long
thought, and I think my position is defined in "The
Bridge Between Two Worlds," that demigods—great
but yet finite beings—had to do with the bringing of
our planet into separate, individual form. This whole
subject, and a reasonable explanation of the many mistakes that we see in the realm of nature, are most
admirably and clearly expressed by our Californian
philosopher, Charles Dawbarn, in his articles on "The
Theology of the Twentieth Century," published in your
issues of Aug. 20, Aug. 27 and Sept. 3 of the current
year. Those familiar with his lucid presentation remember that he makes Great Experimenters use the already
existing materials and forces of the universe for new
formations, and thus accounts for what we see to be
unwise or wrong.

For instance, just as we may put excellent goods,
linings and trimmings into the hands of a dressmaker,

who makes them into an ill-fitting or an unbecoming robe, so these Experimenters out of good material go to work to make a world, and, instead of the result being " very good," it is not as good as it might have been in wiser or more experienced hands.

If our earth only spun round in the same plane as she goes around the sun, then we should not have these violent changes in the seasons, and find that the differ-ence between summer and winter increases as we go from the equator. For instance, in Minneapolis, which is forty-five degrees from the equator, the summers are far hotter and the winters far colder than in northern New Jersey, which is less than forty-one degrees. That is the reason that the Minnesota climate, though stimu-lating at first, exhausts one's vitality after a few years residence there. And, alas! coal, which one can buy here for from four dollars to five dollars, costs there from eight dollars to ten dollars a ton. So the poor must suffer there, and even the rich find it difficult to keep warm when the thermometer registers from zero to ten degrees below zero for three months at a time, as I have known it to do during my residence in Minnesota.

Some of Mr. Dawbarn's Great Experimenters gave great suffering to organic life, when they set the axis on which we revolve awry to the axis of the orbit of the earth. Jupiter tips only a little more than three degrees, while we tip twenty-three and a half degrees. Mars and Saturn tip worse than we do; while the variations in the seasons in Venus and Mercury are so unreason-able that I, for one, am very thankful that my soul did not take embodiment on either one of those intense little planets.

Those Earth Experimenters did us a very poor turn in my opinion, and I hope, Mr. Editor, that when you and I evolve in the course of ages into world-builders, we shall do our work more steadily and more harmo-niously than those who had the handling of the earth.

It is to be hoped that no very orthodox person will have the reading of this letter. I have said to several of them of late that I am very thankful not to be responsible for these great storms and the suffering caused by this intense cold. But it seems to me more tolerable to see suffering caused by the want of care or experience of finite beings than to feel that it is caused by the intentional will and purpose of an Infinite Being, who would be more worthy of love and reverence by making all his creatures bask in happiness and sweet serenity.

The impossibility of harmonizing an omnipotent, predestinating, and infinite personality, who does not work through free agents, with the existence of wrong and pain, has driven many an inquiring soul into atheism. Poor little Wolfgang von Goethe was five when news came of the terrible earthquake at Lisbon, and he pestered and alarmed his young mother by asking how God could be good and allow twenty thousand people to be killed in such a way. She was scarcely out of girlhood herself, being only eighteen when he was born, and of course she could give him no adequate explanation. If she had known that Infinite Power works by finite instrumentalities in *great* things as well as in *small*, she could have quieted his perturbed little mind by an explanation that is comprehensible because it is reasonable.

Yours for humanity and for spirituality.

LETTER FIFTY-ONE.

Vivisection.

December 25, 1898.

To the Editor of THE BANNER OF LIGHT:

I have been puzzled for weeks to know what was the matter with me; but when, during this week, I found myself prostrated, with cold shivers going up and down the spinal column every other day, I submitted to the inevitable, and knew that it was malaria. So I went to the druggist, to consult with him as to the most appropriate poison to fit the case. Quinine was suggested, but rejected on account of its affecting the head, and I can allow nothing to interfere with THE BANNER letters. So I am taking something else, warranted to either kill or cure. If the latter, I will let you know about it next week.

My father, in humorous vein, once said: Man is a biped, but instead of two legs it is two extremes. When he is tired of standing on one of them, he draws it up and puts the other down. To no class of men does this illustration apply better than to the medical profession. If you are writing a story and your hero is ill, just note which quarter of the century he belongs to, learn the medical fad then prevailing, and treat him accordingly.

How well this fact was illustrated by Dr. Bland in two admirable stories published in THE BANNER some time ago! One was laid at the time when blood-letting was the remedy for every disease, and some of his characters lose, or nearly lose their lives, by having the precious life fluid stolen out of their veins. Even the great Washington passed from the mortal plane sooner than needful by being phlebotomized in his last illness.

Each phase in the medical panorama gives place in time to another. Most of these methods have been practiced on the human family alone, but the closing quarter of the nineteenth century has witnessed such appalling and such atrocious tortures inflicted upon helpless brutes in the name of science, as well nigh eclipse the horrors of the Spanish Inquisition. But this atrocity is only another medical fad, and will in time give way to something else.

As a rule, the most earnest advocates of the excising and dismembering practice are the surgeons and doctors about forty years old, though we know of some older doctors who for ambition and to enhance their fame have bowed their knee before this bloody Moloch. But though these excising and dismembering processes are earnestly advocated by surgeons who were graduated fifteen or twenty years ago, we are glad to note that a salutary *reaction* is already setting in, and that the younger surgeons of intelligence and independence who have had the best advantages belong many of them to the reactionary school. They believe that the advantages of vivisection have been enormously exaggerated, and advocate and practice a return to the older and safer process of *assisting* nature rather than attempting to *coerce* her. My acquaintance among surgeons and physicians of the newer schools is not large, but I already know of several, some of whom have studied in Europe and graduated quite lately, who belong to this reactionary class. They will be bitterly opposed by those who belong to the torture school ; but their methods will win, while the cruel ones will die away.

Thirty years ago, if there was knee trouble, the wise surgeons aided nature by protective and ingeniously devised appliances, and in most cases the cure was complete. But these excising practitioners cut the whole joint right out. If the patient has a good constitution he gets over it, but he can never bend his leg again.

One of the trump cards played by the vivisectionists is that if a person's appendix is excised he can never have appendicitis ; and that they have to do it to a great many animals before they dare try it on a human being. And to support their practice, they state that what used to be called enteritis or peritonitis was really appendicitis, and that the patient need not have died if his appendix had only been cut out.

But my learned and "reactionary" friends tell me that when these cases are examined they do not find anything in the appendix at all, and that it is the old-fashioned inflammation of the bowels, caused perhaps by overworking them by excessive and improper food, with the whole human sewage system clogged and unrelieved.

It is reasonable to suppose that when there is an accumulated and undigested mass in the ileac region, it must be difficult to raise it against gravitation into the ascending colon. I should say that flushing the colon in a case like this is far better than to be stretched on a vivisecting table to have one's appendix cut out, after first cutting through the abdominal wall.

Several years ago a young girl went to a hospital to be treated for some local irritation. She was poor and unattended and the surgeons removed bodily the whole of the generative organs, without her knowledge or her *previous consent*. Being healthy, she was recovering, and then learned the terrible thing that had been done to her. She was to have been married immediately after leaving the hospital. She was poor, there was nothing to be done, her life was ruined, she was unsexed.

I suppose the one thing more than another that a human being possesses is his own body. And just as we have the right to use our money while we live, and make such disposition of it after our death as we choose, so have we the right to say effectually what shall and what shall not be done to our body (unless criminals) while living, and to order the disposition of the deserted body after we have ceased using it. If I should have pneumonia, I will not have my pectoral wall cut into, to enable me to breathe a few hours longer by freeing the lungs of some of the pus. All the organs, limbs, and everything else within my epidermis are my own personal possessions, and I will not have them cut into, excised, dismembered, or mutilated in any way, be I alive or dead.

And in the eye of right and justice, every married woman in the world has the same governance over her personal, physical self that a single woman has. When they realize this, and live according to this, a slavery worse than the coolie trade, worse than negro bondage, worse than the chain of the galley slave, will have been brought to an end.

Yours for humanity and for spirituality.

LETTER FIFTY-TWO.

Reunion with Our Loved Ones in the Spirit World.

December 30, 1898.

To the Editor of THE BANNER OF LIGHT :

A lovely kinswoman of mine, quite advanced in years, admitted to me yesterday with some hesitation that she really thinks we may be permitted in the next world to recognize our friends and to enjoy some companionship with them. She said she was brought up to believe that we should not even know each other there on account of being absorbed in God and Jesus. But the sweet thought of seeing the dear ones again, especially her husband, whom she deems far too good for her here, is stealing into her heart, and I could see the result of something I said to her on a previous visit.

I had suddenly said : "Oh, my dear, how happy, *happy*, you will be to meet F—— again !" "Oh, don't !" she said ; but I would go on. "F—— will be so glad to see you, and will love you more than ever, because you were so good to her little boy, whom she had to leave on earth without a mother." F—— was (*is*, I mean) her favorite sister, and her little boy was a cripple. This dear lady keeps aloof from Spiritualism, fearing it is a delusion invented by the Enemy of souls, in order to make those who accept it the future denizens of his dread abode. But the little seeds of hope fly everywhere on angel pinions. and sometimes take root in hearts that we have longed to cheer, but almost lost all hope of doing so.

Of all the exquisite revelations made by this latter day promise of glory, it seems to me that the very dearest is the knowledge that families whose members love each other will be reunited in the spirit-world. And there is no qualification, no reservation, no hesitation in our delight in the thought.

If we ask our church friends if they do not feel sure of meeting those they love again, they hesitate, and temper their reluctant "yes" with an "if." "Yes," they say, "we shall meet each other again, if we are in Christ—if we have given our hearts to the Savior." And the doubt whether they and those they love are really Christians, and the knowledge that many estimable friends are not, makes them walk with downcast eyes and bated breath during their stay on the earth.

It is indeed delightful to get out of "these mists and vapors, these earthly damps," out of the regions of *ifs* and vain wishes, into the clear sunlight of a natural universe. In this universe of nature, being in this body or out of this body makes no difference. If we know and love each other here, we shall know and love each other there. If our sweetest pleasure here is to feel the hand-clasp of affection, and to look love into eyes that look with responsive love into our own, we shall have precisely that pleasure there, for "souls are not denaturalized by death."

Some are so absorbed here in individual love and companionship that they forget to shed the tender sprays of affection on other hearts; they forget to revere those souls who have passed on to higher stages of development; they forget the beneficent plan of the universe, and the unerring sequences of cause and effect. If they continue thus while here, they will be the same there, at least for a while.

But they are not wicked in being and doing so; they are simply undeveloped, and narrower than they will be by and by. Such persons are told by the Church that they are worshiping the created rather than the creator; that God is a jealous God, and that he will take their idol away, and thus force them in anguish to

bow to himself alone.   But these statements are untrue.
Infinite God is far too great, too self-poised, to be jealous concerning the feelings of any finite beings toward
each other.   God, if we allow ourselves to say anything
of what is obviously beyond our finite comprehension,
is the fountain of absolute reason.   God walks a path-
less way beyond any mortal thought, and yet the gleam
of reason that we see in our little individual self is the
earnest of infinite potencies beyond.

Whether here or there, we may enjoy the companionship of those we love, we may give love for love, we may
give worship for worship, for love's own sake.   As we
go on and enlarge our sphere of thought and feeling,
we shall expand toward those bright beings whom we
shall see walking on those supernal heights.   We shall
also come to realize more deeply and assuredly the solid
groundwork of all physical formations, and all spheres
of thought, intellect, and emotion, and the unerring law
that makes the permanent progress of each and all
depend on righteous action, righteous feeling, and
reasonable thinking.

In all these paths of progression, we may sometimes
walk alone.   But in that case, we shall return later to
the companionship of those we love, let them aid us to
climb yet higher, or ourselves stoop to them, and

> "Allure to brighter worlds, and lead the way."

Yes ; intellectual exchange of thought, soul-compan-
ionship, and soul-communion will enhance the pleasure
of action, and sweeten our periods of repose, whether
in the body or out of the body, and this will continue
to be the case just so long as we remain finite.   Should
we ever expand into infinity, should we ever return
ultimately to God, as the sublime Plato expressed it,
we shall be in a condition that we cannot comprehend
now, and we cannot divine whether we shall then want
companionship.

One passing through the seventh decade of human
life naturally (I say naturally, but I cannot answer for
those who have been denaturalized by old dogmas),

naturally longs for the day when he or she will be freed
from the tenement of clay, and pass to the embrace of
those whom he loved so dearly, and then lost for awhile.
When I think that the day is coming when I shall again
be with my father, my mother, and the brother who
was freed in 1896, a feeling of joy comes over me that
is well nigh ecstasy. There are many others I shall be
glad to see, relatives, friends, old comrades and co-
workers ; but these three will be first and dearest—
my father, my mother, Elnathan.

I was ten when my mother died, and we sailed away
that night, leaving her precious form in the bosom of
the lone ocean isle of St. Helena. Before I was eleven
my father sailed again for Burmah, leaving Adoniram,.
Elnathan and me to grow up without a father and a
mother. They were together until after graduation
from college. I was alone. My father died near Burmah
the fourth year after, and there is a little daguerreo-
type of me that he used to cry over.

The year after he was graduated from college Elnathan had a sunstroke, and the fourth year after he was
immured in an insane hospital at the age of twenty-six.
He remained in an insane hospital for *thirty-two years*.
During all those years I never had one pleasure unshad-
owed by his condition. He never lost his memory nor
his individuality, nor the consciousness that he was a
prisoner, immured like a felon, as he bitterly told me.

When he was *fifty-eight* I was allowed to take him to
my home, and we were together the last year of his
earth-life. The last eight months he was all my own.
We were alone together. Love and the knowledge that
he was safe with his sister made him sane. Then he
went to father and mother.

See Elnathan again, dear reader ? Oh, what a happy
day that will be ! Tears of joy fall from my eyes. He
came back to me a feeble, paralyzed old man. When
I see him again he will be young, bright, strong, exquisitely beautiful, and radiantly happy. Our youthful companionship will be restored. We shall gather the wild

roses and the swamp pinks again, and revel in our
favorite authors, some of whom we shall see. Our
parents will smile on our joy.

"Over the river faces I see,
 Fair as the morning, looking for me ;
 Free from their sorrow, grief, and despair,
 Waiting and watching patiently there.

"Father and mother, safe in the vale,
 Watch for the boatman, wait for the sail,
 Bearing the loved ones over the tide
 Into the harbor, near to their side.

"Brother and sister, gone to that clime,
 Wait for the others, coming sometime;
 Safe with the angels, whiter than snow,
 Watching for dear ones waiting below.

"Sweet little darling, light of the home,
 Looking for some one, beckoning, 'Come,'
 Bright as a sunbeam, pure as the dew,
 Anxiously looking, mother, for you,

CHORUS—
"Looking this way, yes, looking this way,
 Loved ones are waiting, looking this way,
 Fair as the morning, bright as the day,
 Dear ones in glory, looking this way."

Yours for humanity and for spirituality.

ABBY A. JUDSON.

www.ingramcontent.com/pod-product-compliance
Lightning Source LLC
Chambersburg PA
CBHW022358020726
47500CB00002B/335